"I think I'm about to shock you, Colleen."

When he continued, his voice was low and rough, almost a rasp. "I planned never to marry. I don't believe in love, not the hearts and flowers kind. But I changed my mind about marriage today. The kids need stability. You love them like I do...."

Colleen sensed what was coming then, but couldn't believe it. Cade was right, he was shocking her.

"I think we should marry, Colleen."

Her heart gave a huge leap. She couldn't move, couldn't speak. This had to be a dream. They barely knew each other—how could they possibly consider marriage?

What kind of man makes the perfect husband?

A man with a big heart and strong arms—someone tough
but tender, powerful yet passionate....

And where can such a man be found?

Marriages made on the ranch...

Susan Fox lives with her youngest son, Patrick, in
Des Moines, Iowa, U.S.A. A lifelong fan of Westerns and
cowboys, she tends to think of romantic heroes in terms
of Stetsons and boots! In what spare time she has, Susan is
an unabashed couch potato and movie fan. She particularly
enjoys romantic movies and also reads a variety of romance
novels—with guaranteed happy endings—and plans to
write many more of her own.

THE WIFE HE CHOSE

Susan Fox

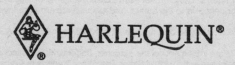

HARLEQUIN®

TORONTO • NEW YORK • LONDON
AMSTERDAM • PARIS • SYDNEY • HAMBURG
STOCKHOLM • ATHENS • TOKYO • MILAN • MADRID
PRAGUE • WARSAW • BUDAPEST • AUCKLAND

ISBN 0-373-03668-X

THE WIFE HE CHOSE

First North American Publication 2001.

CHAPTER ONE

IT HAD taken months to recover from the terrible car crash that had killed her sister. And yet, fully recovering from either her sister's death or her own injuries might never be possible.

Even now, as Colleen James drove down the Texas highway, she suffered the constant ache and weariness of a body that had been broken and traumatized, that was still far from healed after multiple surgeries and months of therapy.

The wreck was also responsible for the frequent headaches she got when she was overtired. She was still weak on her right side, and when she was tired or upset, she was even more unsteady on her feet. The feminine grace and ease of movement she'd taken for granted before the crash were now no more than a golden memory. Her awkwardness embarrassed her. The slim, black cane she hated to use was a necessity and might yet be for weeks or months more.

But the emotional injuries were the most formidable. She couldn't seem to shake the depression that clung to her and made her days gray and trying. The terror of driving a car, or even riding as a passenger in one, had been debilitating. Only after days of determined practice with a rental car had she overcome her fear of driving enough to make the two-hour trip from San Antonio to the Chalmers Ranch.

Because it was imperative that she speak to Cade Chalmers. She'd sent a handful of letters to him, including flowers and condolences for the recent death of his brother, Craig. This past week, she'd phoned him three times, including the call this morning just before she'd left San Antonio. He hadn't responded to any of her letters and he'd never returned her calls.

She'd decided a try at a face-to-face meeting with him was preferable to contacting him through a lawyer, which he might resent, but time was running out.

Her late sister's three-year-old son and infant daughter—had now also lost their father. Craig Chalmers had drowned accidentally a month ago, and permanent custody of the children should soon be decided by a judge. The fact that their Uncle Cade currently had custody of them made it imperative that she speak to him.

Colleen was certain he'd given no thought to her regarding visitation, or that he'd even considered granting her access to her late sister's children. That's why she'd made the difficult trip, to both remind Cade Chalmers that she existed and to demonstrate to him the level of concern she felt about his apparent indifference to preserving the children's tie to her.

She couldn't successfully petition the courts for the privilege of raising them herself because of her limitations, but she wanted to have some part in their lives.

Cade's late brother, Craig, had also been indifferent to her, and he'd blamed her for the fact that she'd enabled Sharon's trial separation from him by allowing her and the children to live with her while they decided whether or not to divorce. His refusal to respond to her letters or calls after Sharon's death was proof of that.

And Colleen had been the one who'd been driving when Sharon was killed. Thank God the children had been safely at home in her apartment with a sitter. There'd been no way to avoid or escape the semi-trailer truck that had all but run over their car in a busy San Antonio intersection. The setting sun had blinded the truck driver to their car until it was too late. His frantic effort to stop the turning vehicle had been hindered by the powerful momentum of the loaded trailer.

Though she remembered nothing of the wreck or that last day with Sharon, she'd later seen the newspaper reports of it that had been saved for her, and the traffic reports, along with the trucker's and witness's statements. The terror she had now was the result of the horrifying nightmares that resulted.

A fresh sheen of perspiration sent a chill over her skin and her palms were suddenly slick on the steering wheel. The two-lane highway in front of her seemed too narrow to safely navigate, and every time she saw a semi hurtling in her direction in the oncoming lane, she felt a jolt of fear. The nausea was overwhelming.

If the turnoff to the ranch hadn't finally come into sight, she might have had to find another place to pull off the highway. What should have been a two-hour trip to the ranch had lengthened to more than four because of the occasional stops she'd had to make to calm herself. There'd been times that day when only her desire to see her niece and nephew again had made her go on.

Once she turned off onto the ranch road, she brought the car to a halt and tried to recover. A headache thumped at her brain, and it seemed to take forever before the nausea calmed. Her hands still trembled and she had a cautious drink of bottled water to soothe her dry mouth.

Finally settled enough to drive on, Colleen started down the ranch road. The car's slower speed on the gravel and the absence of traffic helped put her at ease. Over the last long, slow rise of road, the main house came into view.

The Chalmers Ranch headquarters was impressive, even against the rugged backdrop of massive rangeland. The fact that the Chalmers measured their vast land acres by the tens of thousands was still an overwhelming notion to someone who'd been born and raised in the city.

The main house held its own among the barns and buildings and the network of corrals that spread out behind it. The house was a huge, single-story adobe built in a C that faced away from the road and boasted a red tile roof and a deep front veranda with adobe arches. The shade beneath the veranda roof promised a cool haven from the heat of a Texas afternoon.

By the time Colleen pulled her rented car to a halt near the end of the front walk, she was trembling with nerves. Fortunately, the place looked deserted, which gave her time to blot the perspiration from her face and shore up her courage.

She doubted she'd ever have enough courage to face Cade Chalmers calmly and confidently. Her sister had been intimidated by him, though she'd also confided to Colleen that he'd been gentle and very good to the children. He'd never shown Sharon much warmth or approval, which had made it difficult for Sharon to feel comfortable with him.

Colleen's own memory was of a big, rugged man almost too gruff and terse to approach. In the few times she'd met him, he'd been distant and polite, but his manner suggested he judged people harshly.

He'd made it obvious that he found her uninteresting and inconsequential, perhaps no one he'd even notice if she hadn't been the sister of his brother's wife.

Colleen was hardly the beauty her sister had been and now, with her dark hair a scant two inches long if that, she felt even less attractive than before the crash. She'd lost so much weight that she looked like a plain, effeminate boy. Men had rarely found her attractive and now they virtually ignored her except to stare at her cane and observe her awkward manner with a mix of curiosity and veiled pity.

All of that underscored the notion that little Beau and baby Amy were the only family she'd ever have. And though she'd loved both of them fiercely from birth, the circumstances of her bleak future made it imperative to be allowed access to them and permitted the joy and happy responsibility of being their aunt. She was the only closely related member from the James family that the two children had. Surely Cade Chalmers would see the importance of that.

Cade Chalmers was on his way to the kitchen from his office in the east wing, when he heard the car pull up out front. He walked to the entry hall to see who it was, but he didn't recognize the thin, frail woman who stepped out and started toward the door. The black cane got his immediate attention and memory kicked in.

Colleen James walked stiffly, her every movement giving as much an impression of self-consciousness as of wary care. She used the support of the cane as if she needed it. So much so that he wondered why she was not on crutches.

Colleen was one person he didn't care to see or have anything to do with. She'd let herself get too involved in the petty marital dispute that had resulted in the death of her sister and finally his brother, leaving a three-year-old and an infant orphaned. If she'd refused to let herself get drawn into it all, things might have been quickly resolved. It was his belief that flighty, irresponsible Sharon might have settled down easier to her family responsibilities if Colleen hadn't been around to rescue her whenever she couldn't get her way.

Sharon had been the kind of mercenary female he'd been pushing away all his adult life. His brother had fallen for her then let himself be dragged around like a lovesick fool. Sharon had paid him back by making his life hell.

And that hell had been the litmus test of Craig's level of addiction to his beautiful, manipulative wife. Then she'd had the bad luck to die.

Following the accident, Cade had had a distraught brother to deal with, a bewildered toddler and a helpless infant on his hands. Colleen had been in a coma for weeks so the arrangements for her sister's funeral had also fallen to him.

Craig had learned later that Colleen wanted no part of him or the kids, so Cade had rapidly put her out of his mind. He'd had enough to handle with the kids and the ranch and his younger brother's descent into a bottle. Craig hadn't been able to face life sober without his flighty wife.

But both of them were gone now. Gone and oblivious to the pain and hardship they'd left behind for their kids.

Why Colleen James suddenly decided to show up here was no more than a minor mystery for him. One that would surely take little time to uncover and was sure to amount to nothing of real consequence. Maybe she needed money. If she did, she was out of luck. James women had gotten their last dollar from Chalmers men.

He opened the door just as Colleen stepped into the shade of the veranda. The surprise of his appearance seemed to startle her and she faltered. But then the surprise was his as he saw her up close.

Her skin was pale, nearly translucent, and there were feathery lines of strain around her mouth. Weariness made her eyelids droop slightly, but the look in the clear blue of her eyes was almost spiritless.

She had been willowy before, but now she was thin and about as insubstantial as a strip of gauze. A light breeze would topple her and he was inclined to go easy on her.

His gaze flicked to the car behind her and he revised his impression. She was well enough to drive herself from San Antonio, so she was probably stronger than she looked.

Her sister had tried everyone's patience with a list of minor infirmities that ran the gamut from headaches to frazzled nerves. She'd had a way of avoiding the daily care of her kids that had seemed selfish to him. And though hiring nannies and sitters had been a solution the Chalmers' could easily afford and had, Sharon's penchant for firing them or running them off with demands to lavish her with as much care and attention as they gave the kids, made the search for replacements a constant bother.

But as he stared at the changes in Colleen James, he felt guilty for the harsh comparison. He knew her injuries had been severe and it was obvious she was nowhere near a full recovery. And the frailty he saw would be impossible to fake. Curious now, he studied her more intently.

Her sable hair was too damned short. Short enough that it tried to stick out all over her head, but she'd smoothed it down with some kind of hair goo. Her eyes, a near robin's egg color, were large and fringed with dark lashes. Her nose was fine and slim and her lips were only slightly full, though they looked tender and vulnerable to him—too tender and vulnerable to have had much kissing.

If she ever put on weight, her small body would be more feminine. The image the thought put in his mind startled him and caused a strong stir of attraction in spite of the frail boyish look she had now.

His gruff, "Miz James," was formal and terse.

Her quiet, "Mr. Chalmers," was equally formal,

but he'd seen the quiver of anxiety that showed in her eyes. "May I come in?"

The question acknowledged his rudeness in staring at her, rather than immediately inviting her in. But it was also an acknowledgment of his right to deny her access to his home. Sharon wouldn't have asked. She'd have helped herself and walked in. Or gone teary if she even imagined resistance.

Cade stepped aside to let her pass, then walked through the entry hall at her slow pace. He ushered her into the living room and as she chose a place to sit at the end of the sofa, he called his housekeeper. Esmerelda appeared at once.

"¿Sí?"

"Could you bring in a tray?"

"Coffee?"

Cade glanced at Colleen.

"Just water would be fine, thank you."

His brisk, "And coffee for me, Esmerelda," sent the housekeeper back to the kitchen. Cade took a seat in the big armchair that faced the sofa and watched coolly as Colleen set her cane aside.

"Thank you for seeing me. I was sorry to hear about Craig. It was a shock."

Cade felt a nettle of anger. There'd been no acknowledgment from her of his brother's death until this moment. It was almost as if she'd decided she needed to express her condolences now only because she wanted something from him. And he could tell when females wanted something from him. He could always tell.

She went on and he felt his irritation rise. "I realize the flowers and the card were too late for the funeral, but I didn't find out until I read it in the papers.''

He caught the faint chastisement for not informing her himself, but she wasn't pitiful enough to let her off the hook for lying about flowers and condolences.

"There were no flowers or card, Miz James,'' he said bluntly. "Why are you here?''

Colleen felt the sting of his rebuke, but she was shocked that the flowers and card had not been delivered.

"There must be some mistake. Whatever had happened these past months, Craig was my brother-in-law. I couldn't make it to the funeral, but I did send flowers and a card. I wouldn't have let something that serious go by unacknowledged, even if it was belated.''

Her explanation did nothing but harden his rugged expression, and he'd never seemed more intimidating. His big body was wide-shouldered, narrow-hipped, and corded with heavy muscles that made him rock-solid and gave an impression of physical power that no one but a bodybuilder would dare to challenge.

But it was his face that held her attention, and always had. Rugged and no-nonsense, he had dark brows over deep-set eyes the color of aged bourbon. His cheekbones were high and prominent enough to suggest at least a trace of Native American ancestry. His nose was sharply bladed and gave the same impression of ancestry, but his mouth was a carved line that could go straight and hard with temper or—rarely—curve into a line that lit his face and made him seem years younger and surprisingly handsome.

Because Cade Chalmers was not handsome, not really. But he was impressive and his harsh, rugged looks were as charismatic as a movie star's. It had always been a struggle not to stare at him, but he'd never caught her at it because she'd been virtually invisible to him. A lackluster, unremarkable female firmly in the shade of her beautiful, outgoing younger sister.

She stared at him now, though, almost more than she cared to, because he'd become impatient with her. And he was angry because he thought she'd lied to him.

"Why are you here?" The terse question closed the subject of the flowers and the card. He'd heard her explanation and judged her a liar. Distressed, she rallied to correct the judgment.

"I'm sure the florist kept a record of the order. It was a local shop. Josie's Flowers, I think. And I used my Visa card."

Cade's dark brows lowered. He'd made up his mind and it was clear that he didn't want to be confused by the facts. Colleen felt her dismay deepen. This was a terrible start.

"Is that why you didn't answer my letters or return my calls," she asked cautiously, "because I'd hurt your feelings?"

Because I'd hurt your feelings?

Colleen felt a jolt of horror. She'd not intended to put it that way! As if someone like her could ever be important enough to Cade Chalmers—or that anyone could—to *hurt his feelings* was preposterous.

Offend or insult him, yes; hurt his feelings, no. Men like Cade Chalmers were too macho to own up to feminine notions like hurt feelings. In this case, he'd probably been angered by what he'd consider an intentional snub. She should have worded it that way, but one of her problems after the crash was that she sometimes spoke imprecisely.

To her surprise, the hard slash of his stern mouth relaxed into the suggestion of a smile. His low-voiced, ''What letters?'' was not harsh at all then, as if his amusement over the hurt feelings remark had softened him.

Encouraged and distracted from correcting her remark, she answered. ''Besides the flowers, I sent you three letters asking about the children and a condolence card, and I called here this week and left phone messages three times. One of those times was this morning.''

She hesitated, not certain it was possible that he couldn't have seen or heard about the letters or the calls. Had he truly not received them? Or was he lying? If he was, then his earlier challenge to her honesty gave her grave concerns about his character, and she was suddenly worried about him raising Amy and Beau.

''Mr. Chalmers, I have tried to contact you,'' she said earnestly. ''I know I had the address right and I know I dialed the right number. You should know I have, and I think you probably do.''

Now the faint amusement on his face vanished and his features went harsh again at her quiet conclusion. She was shaking now and she felt tiny dots of perspiration break out on her skin. Nevertheless, she dared a softly spoken, ''I can't imagine why you'd...pretend.''

Unable to bear the sharp look he gave her then, she glanced anxiously away and felt painful heat in her cheeks. Why would he lie to her like this? Obviously he didn't respect her enough or hold her in high enough regard to tell her the truth. The lack of personal integrity that implied increased her worry about the kind of guardian he would make.

Any realistic hope she'd had that he'd allow her to be a part of the children's lives died. And probably had long before the moment she'd questioned his word. Now she'd have to find a lawyer and see what the courts might grant her. And that would probably be nothing.

Before either of them could say more, Esmerelda came in with a tray. Once she set it on the stout wooden coffee table between them, she handed Colleen a heavy crystal glass of ice water. Colleen took it with a faint smile and a word of thanks.

Her hands shook, and the weight of the crystal and the condensation on the outside of the glass made it difficult for her to hold. Esmerelda left the room and once Colleen had taken a tense sip, she leaned forward to put the glass back on the tray, prepared to pursue Cade for an explanation. Though she was wary of him and more than a little terrified, she had to think about little Beau and Amy and their best interests. Nothing was more important than that.

But to her horror, the glass slipped from her weakened grip and dropped to the floor with a sharp crack. Water flew everywhere and the sudden disaster shamed her. Awkwardly, she slid forward on the sofa to reach for the neatly folded linen napkin on the tray. She didn't realize the napkin was anchored by

the saucer of the coffee cup until she yanked on it
and managed to spill the brim-full cup that rested on
its corner.

Mortification and the frantic need to blot up the
mess she'd made on the floor made her lose her balance on the edge of the sofa and go down painfully
on her left knee in the spilled water and ice cubes.
The glass hadn't broken, but her knee grazed it and
sent it spinning under the coffee table.

Cade was at her side almost before she could register the series of minor disasters. He lifted her and
set her out of the way on the sofa. He took the napkin
and calmly blotted water off the carpet with one hand
while he got the glass with the other and swiftly replaced the spilled ice cubes before he set it back on
the tray. At least the rolled edges of the tray had kept
the coffee spill confined.

Colleen's horrified, "I'm so sorry," was as much
as she was capable of. Even if she hadn't already
alienated Cade and spoiled her chances to be allowed
contact with the children, the clumsy weakness she'd
hoped to conceal from him had now been starkly
demonstrated. Her obvious physical difficulties
would make her a poor choice for unsupervised visits
with a toddler and an infant, and Cade Chalmers
would have no patience with the added inconve-
nience her involvement would cause him. If there'd
ever truly been a realistic hope of her involvement.

Evidently, Esmerelda heard the commotion and
came rushing back into the room.

"I'm so sorry for this," Colleen repeated to her.

Esmerelda waved it away with a gracious smile,
as if the embarrassing disaster was too minor to take

note of. "Water on the carpet is not a problem." She started forward to pick up the tray as Cade moved aside.

He addressed Esmerelda before she could. "Do you remember any letters Miz James might have sent?"

Esmerelda seemed to think the question was odd, but she nodded. "*Sí.* I have seen her name on some and also the fine flowers she sent. I put them on your desk like always and the flowers on this table. Do you not recall?"

Cade's face was like weathered rock. "Thanks, Esmerelda. I'd appreciate a new tray when you get this one out of the way."

Esmerelda bustled out and the room went utterly silent. Cade still stood staring at her and she was helpless to do anything but stare at him.

The proof of her honesty was Esmerelda's confirmation about her letters and the flowers. He'd asked his housekeeper about them without seeking a moment alone with her to coach her to lie, so he'd obviously had nothing to hide. And yet, he'd never seen the letters or known who'd sent the flowers. How was that possible?

"My apologies, Miz James." The faint growl in his low voice carried an edge that made him seem both contrite and sincere. "I have no explanation. You sent letters and I didn't read them. And I *would* have read them."

Colleen believed him instantly and felt her tension ease. A little of her hope came back. Perhaps their terrible start wasn't so terrible after all.

"I wanted to know how Beau and Amy are. Craig

never took my calls about them and he never replied to my letters to him because he maybe blamed me for it all. I thought you either felt the same way about me or you were continuing with his wishes.''

It hurt to admit to Cade that his brother had probably hated her and blamed her for everything. And pointing it out to him was also a risk. He might decide to shun her to fulfill his brother's wishes. But she had to be straightforward with Cade. Even if instinct hadn't warned her to do so, she would have felt compelled to tell the whole truth, foolish or not.

Cade sat down then, but his dark gaze never left hers. "Craig said you wanted nothing to do with the kids or him."

The magnitude of Craig's lie was another shock and Colleen felt her face pale. She could tell that it also upset Cade, whose rugged face was now utterly solemn. Worse than questioning Cade's honesty would be to say something that would put his dead brother's honesty into question when he was no longer alive to defend himself. And though she hadn't meant to do that, she had and she was helpless to correct the blunder.

The silence stretched out. She couldn't maintain eye contact with his intense scrutiny and glanced uneasily away, though his gaze had turned disturbingly gentle.

"I'll get to the bottom of the trouble with the letters," he said gruffly. "But you asked about the kids."

His mention of the children brought her hopeful gaze back to his and she couldn't help the swell of longing and emotion she felt. It had been six long months since she'd seen them.

"They're fine. I've got a nanny for them, but it's her day off and a neighbor of mine took them to a friend's house to play."

"Can I see them?" Her breathless question was eager with hope, but she was terrified he'd find some reason to refuse.

"Of course you can." The voice that was big and gruff enough to roar out commands was now husky and surprisingly gentle.

Relief intensified the emotion she felt and she looked down at her shaking hands to get control of the tears that made her eyes feel scalding and full. When she could, she gripped her hands together to still their tremors then gathered her courage and looked over at him.

"Thank you, thank you so much. It means a lot." She smiled at him, but the effort not to cry made her mouth tremble. Desperate to keep from going teary in front of him, she went on with the more difficult reason she'd come to the Chalmers Ranch.

"Obviously, you'll soon petition the court for permanent custody or guardianship of Beau and Amy, if you haven't already. I wanted to be sure you know that I hope to have a place in their lives."

There it was. Plain-spoken and direct. She was putting her heart on the line and praying Cade Chalmers wouldn't break it. It was one thing to let her see the kids today. It was quite another to go on allowing it and to grant her the security of detailing it in a legal agreement.

She could read nothing in the rugged expression

that suddenly shuttered his reaction from her. His low voice went soft, but there was no mistaking the hint of warning.

"Will you challenge me for custody?"

Colleen eased forward on the sofa to lean earnestly toward him. "I want to be assured of a place in their lives. As you can see, I'm not sure a court would consider me physically capable of around-the-clock care for a toddler and an infant. I expect to recover enough to eventually do that, but I still don't know how long that will take."

She paused and saw that his expression had eased a bit. "If the children are safe and well cared for and happy here, I don't want to disrupt that. But I do want access to them. I haven't contacted a lawyer for advice about this, but I'm not sure I'd need to independently petition the court if you'll put something in writing to give me legitimate legal standing. Or whatever the process might be."

Now she saw the glint of wariness in his dark gaze and she rushed to assure him of her good will.

"I'm willing to allow the court to do an assessment of me and my home. I can cover the cost of that."

His look turned sharp and considering. "You're serious about this?"

Emotion rose high at the comment. "I love them very much, Mr. Chalmers. I can't describe how much I've missed them. I came here to make sure you know that I want to have a part in their lives and their upbringing."

"How much a part?" Now his wariness intensified, as if he thought her presence in the children's lives would be intrusive.

"I'm their aunt. I'd like to fulfill the pleasure and responsibility of that relationship. I know I can't demand equal time, but I hope to have regular involvement and maybe the freedom to at least express an opinion about their care and upbringing from time to time."

"You want a lot. What else are you after?"

The question seemed adversarial to her and that was confusing. He'd appeared to soften toward her, but now it seemed that he hadn't softened at all. Maybe he considered her request excessive. She rushed to assure him she didn't intend to cause problems or be a source of trouble.

"You're welcome to select someone of your choice to evaluate me, and if you allow me to frequently visit over whatever time is left before you go to court, you'll be able to see for yourself whether you think I'm a good or bad influence on them. And it's not my intention to be an adversary or to be in competition with you. I just want to have a good relationship with my family."

"What about money?"

Colleen felt the blunt question impact her, but she didn't understand it at all. Had she missed something? But then she realized what he meant and reached for her handbag.

"I could write you a check now as a deposit on the cost of the evaluation," she said hastily as she took out her checkbook and opened it to take hold of the pen hooked on the check register. Pen poised to write, she glanced over at him. "How much do you think? Five hundred? A thousand?"

A look of astonishment crossed his harsh expression and that confused her even more. Why did he look so surprised? She'd already told him she could cover the cost of the evaluation. Did he not want a professional evaluation of her suitability to have contact with the children?

The awful feeling that she'd missed something important in their conversation both shamed and stunned her. Her worries over her sometimes imprecise word choices suddenly seemed minor in the face of having failed to follow the details of this conversation. What had she missed? She hadn't been aware of this problem before and the idea distressed her.

The sound of a car pulling in behind her rental car out front distracted them both. Cade immediately got up and strode toward the entry hall. Colleen forgot her worry over the confusing turn of conversation. This might be Cade's neighbor bringing the children home and she felt a thrill of excitement.

Revived, she left her handbag and checkbook on the sofa, got carefully to her feet, and ran nervous fingers over her hair to make certain it was still tamed. She got her cane and prepared to walk toward the entry hall the moment she heard the sound of the children.

She was so weary from the long drive and the tension of her difficult talk with Cade that she'd wondered how much longer she could last and still get back to the motel where she would rent a room for the night.

But knowing that the children were probably home

and that she was about to see them and hold them and kiss them, excited her and gave her an almost giddy energy that more than revived her flagging strength. She didn't have long to wait.

The front door barely had time to open before she heard Beau's high young voice.

"Uncle Cade! Lori's kids got puppies!"

Colleen made her way to the entry hall, her heart going wild with excitement. It'd been six months. How much bigger had Beau grown? Would he still remember her? And Amy! She'd been five months old back then, so now she was almost a year old. Was she walking? How many words could she speak?

Colleen stepped into the entry hall, unable to keep a wide smile off her face. Because she had eyes only for the children, she barely noticed the slim, elegant blonde who ushered Beau inside and carried little Amy on her shapely hip.

Beau had indeed grown and the sight of him made her eyes sting. But Amy looked more like a little girl than a baby now, and her blue sundress set off her dark coloring and blue eyes. Beau's dark hair was mussed, his shirttail was out and he looked like he'd been playing in the dirt.

They were so beautiful and so perfect that she had to blink away happy tears to keep her eyes from blurring and missing a second of the sight of them.

Beau saw her first as she stood there, hoping and yearning, careful to stay at the edge of the commotion while she waited for some sign of recognition and welcome from them. The way she felt now, she wasn't certain how long she could keep herself from grabbing them for hugs and kisses, but she could do nothing until she was sure she wouldn't startle either of them. After all, she looked different, and the last thing she wanted to do was upset them and make them wary of her. And it had been so long!

She smiled at Beau who'd stopped in his tracks and was staring at her. Amy had caught sight of her, too, and her wide eyes gave her a good looking over. She knew Amy had been too young when she'd last seen her, but she expected that Beau would remember, though she worried that her injuries might have changed the way she looked too much for him to recognize her quickly.

To her utter dismay, Beau's happy smile froze then fell away. The look on his face switched to a frightened frown and he went instantly to Cade and grabbed his leg for security. Cade reached down to ease the boy away enough to pick him up. Beau's little arms latched around his neck and his small face paled.

Sensing that something was terribly wrong, Colleen tried a soft, "Hello, Beau. You remember your auntie, don't you? Aunt Colleen?" She took a small careful step forward, but Beau cuddled closer to Cade's neck and eyed her mistrustfully.

Cade looked as if he thought Beau's reaction was strange but he gave the boy a small bounce to draw his attention. "Your auntie's come a long way to see you and your sister, squirt."

"I don't wanna see her."

His little voice seemed to echo in the open hall and Colleen was stricken with hurt. She tried not to show it, but her smile faded a little. The entry hall had gone quiet. Colleen was aware of nothing except Beau's fearful little face and the way Cade studied him.

"Why not?" Cade made the question sound light, but Colleen understood how serious it was. And that her future access to the children rested on Beau's answer.

Beau didn't hesitate. His small face was solemn and certain.

"Because she killed my mommy and hurt me an' Amy."

Cade's dark gaze streaked to hers and she felt the impact as she saw him close his mind to her. She couldn't speak a word in her defense because she was strangling and couldn't get a full breath. It was as if the air had suddenly been sucked from the room.

And then the room began to move. Dizziness made it difficult to stand with just the support of the cane, so she put out her free hand—her weaker right hand—to the wall to keep herself upright.

Cade said something then to the woman, but Colleen's ears were suddenly filled with a roaring sound. He set Beau on his feet. The moment he did, Beau ran out of the foyer through the passage opposite the one she stood next to. The woman walked past her silently with little Amy, but Colleen was too dazed, too horrified to move.

She killed my mommy and hurt me an' Amy.

The terrible words and the frightened look on Beau's face shook her and made her doubt her sanity. Somehow she'd fallen into some strange nightmare. A strange, horrible nightmare.

She felt her knees begin to give way, but the gray haze that suddenly blanketed her vision and went black kept her from knowing whether she hit the cool hard tile of the entry hall or not.

CHAPTER TWO

COLLEEN awoke alone in a dim, cool bedroom. A light blanket covered her from chin to ankle. Her head was pounding and the ringing in her ears made her feel nauseous.

And then it all came back to her. Little Amy and Beau, so beautiful. At last she could see them, was inches from touching them, kissing their sweet cheeks and hugging them to her heart.

But then the fright in Beau's face and the horrid words, *She killed my mommy and hurt me an' Amy.*

Colleen rolled painfully to her side and curled up stiffly against the agony.

…and hurt me an' Amy.

The words beat at her brain and pummeled her heart. She'd not harmed a hair on either child. Ever. She couldn't fathom the accusation, but the look in Beau's eyes as he'd said it was utterly sincere. Beau believed it completely. And from the look on Cade's face, he'd believed it, too. Oh, God!

Suddenly she felt profoundly and urgently sick. She wrestled weakly with the blanket and got free. Making her way to the private bath was a larger challenge. She couldn't find her cane, she was almost too weak and uncoordinated to walk, but she was desperate not to be sick before she could make her way from one piece of furniture to another and reach the bathroom.

29

The door to the hall opened, but she was so focused on getting to the bathroom in time that she was only marginally aware of it. She gasped when big hands closed around her waist and Cade's big body pressed against hers. He had her in the bathroom in an instant, sitting her carefully on the edge of the bathtub before he flipped on the light.

"Are you sick?"

His big voice was low and gruff, but he lifted the lid and seat of the commode to accommodate her.

Her panted, "Yes—please leave," was slurred.

"The doctor's on his way," he told her and she felt his big hand settle gently on her shoulder. "Forget about me and get it over with."

Her desperate, "No—leave!" was all she could get out before she was violently ill.

Through every mortifying moment, Cade Chalmers steadied her. Until the sickness was gone and she was limp with cold tears running down her cheeks.

Shame burned over her body and made her skin feel on fire. A cool wet washcloth moved gently and competently over her face. She was too weak and demoralized to resist as Cade helped her to the sink and guided her through a brief routine with a new toothbrush he'd loaded with gel toothpaste.

When she'd recovered and finished freshening up, the quiet consideration Cade had demonstrated—the persistently gentle way he'd taken care of her—made an impression that went so deep in her soul that her heart ached.

The most painful and trying times of her life, especially after the accident, she'd endured alone.

The solitary circumstances of her life meant that once she was released from the hospital, she'd truly been on her own. She had neighbors and friends who sometimes ran errands and looked in on her, but never anyone who stayed and took care of her. Never anyone to relieve the loneliness and despair of long, gray days and painful, restless nights.

After what Beau had said, Cade must loathe the very sight of her. It said something admirable about his character that he was capable of treating her humanely, even though he must despise her.

She could barely stand and leaned heavily against the counter by the sink, her hands braced on the smooth surface.

"I never hurt them, Cade," she got out, unable to stop the tears, though she did her best to keep the sobs quiet.

"Something's wrong here," he growled. "Let's get you back to bed and we'll figure it out later."

He eased her away from the counter and leaned close so he could keep his arm around her waist and gently grip her left arm to support most of her weight.

"I caught you when you fainted and carried you in here, but will I hurt you if I pick you up now?"

"I can walk."

He stopped them both. "That's no answer."

And then he released her arm and bent down to carefully pick her up. The sound of distress she made caused him to hesitate, as if he was afraid he'd hurt her.

"Let me walk. Please."

But Cade must have decided that picking her up

could be done without hurting her because he lifted
her into his arms and held her securely against him.
She looked up into his face to discern the reason for
his calm kindnesses, but his expression was solemn
and hard, though his dark eyes were surprisingly gentle.

His gaze shifted from hers and he started for the
bedroom and the bed. He set her on the edge of the
mattress, then reached behind her to get the blanket
that was bunched and twisted.

"Go ahead and lie back."

Colleen shook her head. "I'd like to sit up."

Cade showed a trace of impatience as he straightened.

Her soft, "I'm fine now," was a lie, but she was
ashamed to let him treat her with such care when it
was probably the last thing he might want to do.

He opened the blanket and wrapped it warmly
around her. Then he moved away from the bed to
drag a nearby wing chair closer. Without asking, he
bundled her onto it. Colleen sank back, grateful for
the cocooning feel of the big chair.

Cade straightened, but his dark gaze never left
hers. Colleen flinched from his scrutiny.

"I'm sorry for the trouble. I'll be fine in a while,
then I can be on my way."

His big voice was terse. "Just like that? Just
leave?"

She looked at him warily, confused by his curt-
ness. "I have no explanation for what Beau said. I
don't even know how I can defend myself. And he
was so...afraid of me." She glanced away and
gripped the blanket to keep from crying. Her heart

was breaking and she was too weary and wrung out to begin to make sense of it all.

"Soon as the doctor looks you over, Esmerelda will get you something to eat, then I'll talk to Beau while you rest. You can have this room."

Colleen shook her head. "I'll stay at that motel back toward town."

"Let's see what the boy has to say first."

She looked up at him. "I'd rather go before your talk. I can't wait around hoping, only to have it go even more wrong later."

"If you're innocent, why would it go wrong?" His eyes had narrowed on her. He suspected her and it surprised her to realize he was trying to hold back judgment.

"I am innocent, but my word is already tarnished because Beau clearly believed what he said. It would be wrong for you to not take it seriously. It may not be possible to prove or disprove anything tonight. And because you can't, it's not responsible of either of us for me to stay around. You have my home address if someone needs to question me."

"Even if everything checks out with the doctor, you're in no shape to drive."

And his mention of the doctor—again—made her feel worse. "Please call the doctor and cancel this. It's not necessary."

"Too late."

Colleen shook her head, and tried not to flinch at the pain that caused her. "Then I'll pay for it. This is a lot of fuss for nothing. I'm sorry you've gone to so much haste."

She cut herself off, appalled at using the wrong

word, then got out the right one. *"Trouble.* Sorry for your *trouble."*

Now she was emotional again. And exhausted and heartsick and scared. "I should have stayed in San Antonio and left things alone. They've been through so much, especially Beau. He shouldn't have had to go through this, too."

She paused and struggled to get control, desperate to hide the fact that she was heartbroken. "They looked beautiful and happy." She looked up at him bravely. "You've done a good job with them and I'm very glad. Relieved." Her voice broke on the word.

Cade stared. Colleen was distraught and clearly devastated. Instinct told him she was incapable of harming anyone, especially the kids. He already suspected why Beau had said what he had, but he needed to be certain.

Moment by moment, Colleen James was becoming more genuine to him. She was nothing like her selfish sister. In his experience with females, Colleen was a novelty. Simple, uncomplicated. And utterly in love with those kids. He suddenly realized that she was the kind of woman who would sacrifice herself for their well-being and happiness if need be, and Cade Chalmers found women like that irresistible.

The faint chime that carried down the hall in this wing of the house told him the doctor had arrived, so he started out of the room.

Colleen submitted to Dr. Amado's brief examination. She knew she'd overdone it that day and the doctor gently chided her for it, though he pronounced her well enough, and readily agreed that her fainting spell was likely the result of being overtired then sustaining an emotional shock. She wasn't comfortable discussing the reason for the shock with him and he didn't press her.

He was kind and took his time, asking about her injuries and the types of physical therapy she'd done, then reminiscing about a couple of the surgeons she'd had. Somewhere along the line it occurred to her that he was stretching out the exam which, by itself, would have taken almost no time.

Just when she was trying to find a way to let him know she suspected him of doing just that, he smiled at her as if he'd read her mind.

"Cade wanted me to keep you busy in here for a while, but it's been pleasant talking to you, Colleen. You're lucky you're doing so well, though it might not seem that way to you right now. Take care of yourself and keep up with the therapy. One day, this will all be in the past." He leaned forward to touch her shoulder. "And she'll live happily ever after."

The small bit of whimsy made her force a small smile because that was the expected reaction. But she had little confidence in happily-ever-after, and today had only confirmed her pessimism.

"How much do I owe you, Doctor?"

"Cade already took care of it, and you'll waste valuable energy arguing with him about it." He gave her a stern look. "And you shouldn't drive anywhere until at least tomorrow, after you've rested up. San Antonio is a long way off when you don't feel well. As you probably discovered today. Go ahead and have a nap before supper. I'll tell Cade to wake you in a couple hours.''

With that, he stood up from the chair he'd dragged over by hers and bid her a pleasant goodbye before he returned the chair to its place, got his medical bag and left the bedroom.

Once she was alone, Colleen made her way carefully to the hall door. San Antonio was indeed too far for her to drive now, but the motel she'd passed earlier that day was probably no more than five miles away. As soon as she found her cane and handbag, she'd be on her way.

Whatever Cade thought he could learn from Beau, Colleen knew nothing would solve Beau's fear of her quickly. It was better for the boy and better for them all if she just gave up and got out. Hadn't she known all along that this had been a wild risk, that it could go wrong?

Though she'd never imagined anyone but Cade Chalmers would be the cause of a new disaster, she shouldn't have come here. As long as she hadn't known for sure that she would never see the children again, she'd been able to have hope. Now she had nothing.

Cade watched Beau run out to join his sister on the back patio. He was on his trike in a flash, then pumped the pedals eagerly to race around the edges of the paving stones that formed the open-air patio that was closed in on three sides by the house.

Amy sat in the center of the patio beneath a leafy trellis in a patch of shade with a stack of oversize plastic blocks. She burst into a wide smile as she watched her brother pedal around on his "race-track."

The "man-to-man" talk he'd had with Beau cleared things up, but Cade felt fresh disappointment in his brother. Craig had told Beau that his Aunt Colleen had killed his mother and because Sharon's death had devastated their little family, it meant that Colleen had also hurt Beau and Amy.

"Daddy said she hurt me and Amy most," Beau had told him. And Craig had apparently told the boy that frequently. It would have been a lie shocking enough to forever silence the boy's worried questions about Colleen after the wreck, and its repetition had also worked to put a fear of her in the kid. Colleen hadn't deserved that.

Craig hadn't been in his right mind when he'd lied to Beau. He'd become irrational about everything and tried to drown his bitterness in liquor, only to end up drowned himself.

The pain of his brother's death a month ago was still a shock, still fresh and raw and agonizing. His pain was compounded by the fact that Craig had lied to him about Colleen from the first, then had deliberately damaged her in Beau's eyes. The injustice of it stunned him.

His part in his brother's lie made him feel sick. He'd easily believed Craig's story about Colleen's wishes after her sister's death, so he'd not bothered to find out the truth for himself. He hadn't known enough about her to question it. He'd based his opinion of her on his opinion of Sharon.

And even he had resented that Colleen had become such a frequent refuge for Sharon. It shamed him to realize that they'd left her lying in a hospital for months, severely injured and grieving her sister, with no family left to console or care for her. He and Craig had virtually abandoned her, and the remorse he felt for that pressed heavily on his conscience.

At least he'd done something to turn things around today. Finally. After he'd gotten answers from Beau, he'd explained to the boy that his daddy was wrong, the wreck had been an accident caused by someone else. And because Colleen hadn't hurt their mother, she wasn't at fault for the hurt to him and Amy.

As usual, he wasn't certain he'd explained things well enough to the boy. Beau wouldn't turn four for another few months, and though he was very bright, he was still a little boy.

He'd finally sent Beau out to play with the gentle encouragement to think about his aunt and see what he could remember about her.

After every one of Sharon's frequent trips to San Antonio with the kids, Beau had come home full of happy stories about the things they'd done with Colleen, so the boy couldn't have forgotten those. Those times, Cade had listened to Beau with only half an ear, more interested in the kid than in the aunt. But today changed all that. If Beau could remember, the problem would be solved.

He heard Doc Amado come down the hall outside his office. Cade turned from the patio doors, relieved to see the doctor's calm smile, and eager to hear whatever doctor/patient privilege didn't prohibit.

Colleen got her handbag and checkbook from the sofa, then found her cane on the table in the entry hall. By the time she stepped out of the house, her tired body felt as if she'd been beaten.

She saw the car that must belong to Dr. Amado, and carefully managed to walk to her rental. Once she opened the door and got in to put her seatbelt on, she was weary beyond belief.

Summoning strength from somewhere, she started the car and put it into gear to head down the long gravel drive to the highway. Because she was over-tired, the ride to the motel seemed even more har-rowing and exhausting than the trip from San Antonio, and it seemed to take forever to get there.

She was grateful when the desk clerk helped her carry her overnight case into the ground-floor motel room he'd rented to her. Once she dug out a tip and handed it over, she didn't have enough energy to even undress. As soon as the clerk stepped into the hall and closed the door, she dragged down the cov-erlet and crawled painfully into bed.

Cade stood by impatiently as he waited for the desk clerk to unlock the door to Colleen's room. They'd tried pounding on the door twice, but there'd been no response and Cade pictured one grim scenario af-ter another.

Colleen had slipped out of the house and he hadn't noticed until he'd gone to her room almost two hours later to look in on her. When Dr. Amado left his office to start back to town, Cade had gone out to be with the kids, never thinking Colleen wouldn't be resting as the doctor had ordered.

The doctor had probably figured the same thing, and hadn't realized the significance of her missing

rental car. He might have assumed Cade had someone move it to the garage.

At last the door was open and the light was on.
Colleen lay on the bed only partially covered, but
still in her clothes. Her athletic shoes were still on
her small feet, as if she'd either been too weary or
too insensible to take them off. He could see from
where he stood just inside the door with the clerk
that she was breathing normally. He handed the clerk
a large bill to both thank him and get rid of him.

"Thank you, Mr. Chalmers. You think she's okay?
Does she need an ambulance?"

"I don't think so, Ronnie." He glanced at the kid.
"I'll take it from here, thanks."

The clerk got the message and left. Cade looked
over at Colleen and walked to the bed.

One strip of Velcro on her shoes had pulled loose
and was now stuck to the edge of the light blanket
beneath the coverlet. The mussed bedding was evidence that Colleen might have been restless with
pain, but too exhausted to fully wake up.

He reached down for the small sneakered foot that
had got Velcroed to the blanket. He peeled open the
other shoe tabs and took the shoe off. The other shoe
came off just as quickly and he tossed both aside
before he bent over her to straighten the covers.

It struck him that she slept like the kids, when they
ran out of steam before a nap and fell instantly asleep
wherever they were, still in their play clothes. The
similarity made him feel tender toward her.

He remembered her look of confusion before she'd
pulled out her checkbook and offered to write *him* a
deposit check for a professional evaluation of her.

She'd been as guileless as a child and clearly oblivious to his question about money. Instinct told him she hadn't faked a second of it. He was still taken aback by that, but it fit with the way she suddenly reminded him of the kids.

Cade didn't know how she should lie to minimize her discomfort, so he didn't dare move her. She was now half on her left side, half on her stomach, and maybe she had some comfort in that position because she didn't so much as twitch. Just like Beau and Amy when they were heavily asleep.

He hated to leave her alone here, but he had no right to take her back to the ranch when she desperately needed rest. His gaze caught on the car rental key next to the lamp on the bed table. He found a sheet of motel stationery in a drawer and scrawled a note that he propped up on the counter by the sink in the bathroom.

Cade took a last look at Colleen and decided she was sleeping naturally. Since she seemed to be all right, he couldn't justify lingering. He had to get back to the kids so Esmerelda could go to a family wedding shower. The nanny wouldn't be home tonight until long after the kids' bedtime.

And though he was aware he'd trespassed on Colleen's privacy, it made him uneasy to leave her. At least he'd solved the problem of her starting for San Antonio in the morning before he could get back here to talk to her. And that didn't make him uneasy at all.

Muscle spasms brought Colleen awake that next morning. The battle was always to get out of bed and walk off the pain before the spasms worsened. If not for the pain, she might have lain in bed hours longer because waking up meant she had to face another hard, disappointing day.

Remembering what had happened with little Beau made this day stretch impossibly long before her. How many more difficult, joyless days could she face? So far they'd been a test of endurance as she'd slowly worked toward her goal.

But now the goal that had drawn her on when she was most discouraged and hurting, had been lost. She had to find a way to move forward without it, to fix something else in her mind that held the promise of home or belonging.

The world was a lonely, unloving place. She was a lonely woman with no one to love and no purpose beyond herself. Surely there was some way to connect, someone or some cause to pour herself into. But she was no good to anyone like this and it might be a long time before she was recovered enough to have anything of value to offer others.

Perhaps she'd take a few college classes in the fall. The trucking company whose driver was responsible for the crash had made a very substantial settlement offer to avoid going to court. She hadn't accepted it yet, since she wanted to be certain it was enough to cover ongoing medical care. And she wasn't yet certain of the level of permanent disability she'd have to cope with, or whether she'd need more education to do another job.

She'd worked as a bookkeeper, but so far, she hadn't been released to go back to the office. And she was afraid she wouldn't be able to do the job now. Recovering her math skills had been frustratingly slow because of her head injury. She couldn't even reconcile her checkbook yet and sometimes she despaired of ever again making consistent sense of complicated math calculations.

It made her worry that she'd fail the college courses. Her confidence was shaky and she was still too fragile to face the challenge of retraining for a new job or learning something new.

Colleen leaned heavily on her cane and braced her weaker right hand against the wall, then along the desk and armoire as she walked painfully up and down the room to stop the spasms and reclaim some semblance of supple movement before she tried to undress and take a shower.

When she at last was able to walk into the bathroom, she caught sight of the note propped up beside the sink.

She instantly recognized the handwriting she'd never seen before only because it so clearly indicated the forceful personality of the man who'd written it.

I'll return your keys at breakfast. Cade.

The peculiar sensation that went through her sent a tingle over her skin. Cade Chalmers had been in her room and she'd never known it. He'd come after her and taken something of hers hostage to enforce his will.

Colleen stared at the note. The sheer novelty of Cade's minor pursuit was dangerous for someone like her. She'd moved in and out of the lives of most of the people around her all her life and was accustomed to the indifference of those who neither objected to her presence nor seemed particularly bothered by her absence. She was not a woman who tried to be noticed, either by her entrances or her exits or in her daily life, and she was too unremarkable to believe that would ever change, though she sometimes fantasized that it might.

Sharon had attracted all the attention there was to be had for the James sisters, and lackluster Colleen had existed at the edge of her sister's beauty and sparkling personality without a single resentment or second thought.

Not that she hadn't wished that, just once, someone would notice her and single her out for the attention Sharon received as naturally as air and sunshine.

Cade's intention to keep her from leaving and this note were hardly a fulfillment of that silly, secret wish, but it was a nice surprise to have a small taste of what it might be like.

Suddenly annoyed with herself, Colleen set the note aside. It was more likely that she'd angered him by slipping away from the ranch. He was too domineering and probably too controlling to tolerate a nobody like her sidestepping his wishes.

And nothing could have happened to explain or resolve Beau's feelings toward her this soon. It was even possible that Cade would have her investigated for child abuse. His taking her car keys had to be the result of his decision to either start the wheels in motion for that or to officially issue a stern edict to her in person that would forever forbid her access to Beau and Amy.

Suddenly so disheartened and depressed that she could barely move, Colleen had to force herself to shower and dress to prepare for a new disaster.

CHAPTER THREE

CADE knocked briskly on the motel room door and waited. When Colleen opened it, she looked flustered and not ready for company. She'd showered and dressed and put on a touch of makeup, but her rapidly drying hair was proof she hadn't tamed it yet. As he'd suspected, without some kind of hair goo, her hair stood straight out all over her head just like Beau's and Amy's had as babies before it got long enough to lie flat.

Obviously, a night's sleep had done her good. She looked fresher than she had yesterday, though there was still a pained weariness about her and he couldn't have missed the anxiety in her eyes.

She didn't greet him and he said nothing to her, but she stepped back and he walked into the room. He could feel her uncertainty, her wariness, and he got the impression that she was terrified of being further hurt and traumatized.

"H-how are Beau and Amy?"

The self-conscious way she asked about them suggested that the only topic that would ever be truly important or significant to her was the kids and how they were. Was that true? But one look at her face told him it was. She was deeply uneasy, which told him how worried she still was about Beau's reaction to her yesterday.

"They're fine. Playing on the patio with Connie

45

when I left." He paused when he saw that she was alert to his mention of a stranger's name. "She's the nanny."

Colleen glanced away and gave a stiff nod. "Did you have a chance to talk to Beau?"

Now he heard the faint tremor in her voice and he was blunt to spare her further suspense. "Craig convinced Beau that Sharon's death hurt them all, Beau and Amy most. Beau was never saying that you did him or Amy any physical harm."

Colleen's gaze veered back to his and held. The hope he saw in her now touched him, so he told her the rest. "Craig was bitter when Sharon left and then went crazy when she was killed. You were handy to blame."

He felt a pinprick of disloyalty to Craig, as if he'd switched sides to stand with an outsider. And a female outsider at that. But the truth was, Colleen James was one female who deserved to have someone on her side. He hoped he was right, but God help her if he wasn't.

Colleen stared at Cade, stunned by the confession and the significance of both the fact that Cade had told her this and the fact that he was virtually pronouncing her innocent of blame. His low voice was gruff and sincere.

"I apologize for Craig," he said and then his voice went softer and kinder. "And I apologize for never bothering to find out the truth. Neither of us should have left you in that hospital alone. There was no excuse for that."

Colleen's heart trembled as the words tumbled over her. Suddenly she was shaking and the sting in her eyes was so sharp and urgent that she turned and took a few steps away. Months of pain and loneliness and despair overwhelmed her, and it was several moments before she was certain she wouldn't cry.

Neither of us should have left you in that hospital alone. There was no excuse...

It was a staggering admission and completely unexpected. And so welcome that it blunted some of the agony of being abandoned. It would be natural to be bitter, to spurn Cade's apology, to spite him for offering a mere apology in exchange for the emotional pain the Chalmers' indifference had inflicted on her.

But the fact that Cade had humbled himself this far was monumental. Both Chalmers brothers had an arrogance about them that made apologies as difficult to imagine from them as it might be rare to witness one.

It amazed her now to realize that she'd thought Cade Chalmers that arrogant. Because he was not. At least not now. And though the confession must have been difficult for him, he'd done it. Her assessment of him as an honorable man rose. She was finally able to find her voice.

"Thank you."

Tears threatened, but she was still faced away from Cade, so she had a few moments to compose herself.

"What h-happens now?" She got the question out because she had to know what all this meant. She was terrified to hope, but she desperately needed to hope. Beau and Amy were the most precious people in a life that, these days, was too often difficult to bear. And she needed to hear from Cade precisely how much of the children's lives she could share.

"What happens now is that you and I go to the restaurant down the highway and, over breakfast, we come to an agreement that's good for the kids and satisfies us both."

Cade made it all sound practical, matter-of-fact and easy. Colleen turned toward him. His rugged face was harshly set, at odds with the mellow timbre of his low voice.

And satisfies us both. Which implied that he placed her approval equal to his own. She'd never once let herself imagine that her wishes about the children would ever be anything more than a distant consideration compared to Cade's. Granting her even a small consideration was more than she'd realistically expected. After all, he didn't have to be bothered with her if he didn't want to be.

Her soft, "Do you really mean that?" was daring, but she hated the almost pitiful uncertainty in her voice.

"Come to breakfast with me and see."

The promise that implied sent excitement skittering through her. And there was something tantalizing and almost playful about the way he'd said it, though his stern features hadn't softened at all. Confused by what she interpreted as a contradiction, she stared.

"Something wrong?" The blunt question sent a flush over her skin.

"No, I'll...I need to get ready." Colleen gripped her cane and moved forward to the bathroom. Cade stepped aside to let her pass.

She hastily misted her hair with the small water

bottle she'd packed, then ran her comb shakily through the short dampened length. She rubbed a dab of mousse between her palms, then combed her fingers through her hair. She'd just picked up her hair dryer when she caught sight of Cade in her peripheral vision.

Colleen glanced self-consciously toward where he stood leaning against one side of the open doorway watching her. Cade's face was as stern as ever, but his voice was low and mild.

"Just interested in the process. I usually only get to see the result."

Colleen felt another flash of heat and turned her attention back to drying her hair. Cade Chalmers was the kind of man women worked hard to attract. Women who'd be perfectly made up and turned out, but expertly, so they'd look naturally gorgeous. Then again, probably all of the women Cade went out with would be gorgeous with or without making an effort.

Colleen knew she'd never be a beauty. Indeed, there was only so much she could do with her unremarkable looks, so she'd never be in the class of women Cade Chalmers would be interested in. Nevertheless, she couldn't help the strange thrill she felt at knowing he wanted to watch her do this small thing.

When she finished, she rapidly gathered her minor collection of toiletries and put them in her cosmetics case. Cade moved obligingly out of the doorway and she walked past him to go to the bed and put the last of her things in her suitcase. She glanced his way.

"Would you mind carrying my suitcase to the car? I already did the express checkout."

Cade came forward and picked up the suitcase. He indicated that she should lead the way, but he reached ahead of her to open the door and waited while she walked out of the room ahead of him.

Once they reached the parking lot, Cade tripped the power locks on the large luxury car parked next to hers, then opened the trunk and put her suitcase inside.

Her soft, "Wait," went ignored as he stepped over to unlock her rented car, wedged the key above the visor, then locked the door and closed it.

Colleen stared at him, shocked and helpless to have either anticipated this or prevented it.

"I'll drive you to San Antonio when you're ready," he told her as he turned back to his car. "I already notified the rental agency to pick it up here."

"I can drive myself," she told him, baffled by his action.

"Another time. Come here and get in."

Colleen stood frozen and now uneasy. She wasn't accustomed to anyone taking over. The mistrust and wariness she felt made her suspicious of this. And she'd lost control of so many things in her life that Cade's takeover made her deeply anxious.

"I want to drive my own car."

Cade's gaze was calm. "I know you do, Colleen, but I'm not sure you should. And you don't have to."

"It's my deci-cision." The small stutter was revealing and she felt embarrassed.

Cade stared, a little surprised at her resistance, but then he had a flash of insight. Colleen was afraid of him and she mistrusted his motives. And she had pride. Perhaps the kind of pride that going through hard times by herself had conferred, but pride nonetheless. He should have considered that.

It was then that he realized that driving herself from San Antonio might have been some sort of milestone for Colleen. One that had taken six months of recovery to achieve.

And yet, in his opinion, she'd not truly been ready to be behind the wheel of a car. She was stiff and awkward, and he couldn't believe her reflexes were what they ought to be. He remembered when she'd dropped the water glass. It had flustered her into a minor series of tiny accidents, so she wasn't truly well enough to be driving a car.

But she'd wanted to see the kids, make sure they were all right and ask to be part of their lives. He knew she'd told him the truth about that. She'd believed he was ignoring her efforts to contact him, so she'd probably thought she had no choice but to drive so far alone. The notion sent a soft trickle of warmth through his chest.

"Come here, Colleen." He kept his voice calm and made sure it was gentle. He thought for a moment that she'd refuse, but then she walked forward, though she stopped a stiff distance from him.

"Why did you do this?"

He heard the anger in her quiet voice. "Because you don't have to be so independent now. Driving a car will be easier and safer for you a few weeks down the line. But not today. I'll drive you today."

Colleen glanced suddenly away from him, her expression troubled. Her small fingers fidgeted with the head of the cane she leaned on and her face flushed.

He studied her tense profile and saw tears gather, then watched as she stubbornly blinked them back. She clearly didn't know how to cope with him and he could feel her frustration.

"Trust me a little, Colleen. I think you trust me with the kids, so trust me with this. This is no shame to you and it's not meant to be."

Now she looked over at him and he could see she was trembling.

"What you're saying is that you think I'm irresponsible. And maybe you think I'm weak or that a woman like me would be grateful to have some big, macho man swoop in and take over. But you're wrong."

Her quiet fierceness shocked him and though his perception of her was evolving more favorably by the second, this was completely unexpected. Women rarely objected to being rescued and pampered. Not the ones in his experience. Most of those played the part to get his attention. He was big and male, single and *rich*. A target for helpless damsels with designs on his money. But not this one, who ironically was a genuine damsel in distress.

Colleen's too thin body was as weak and precarious as a small child's, and she was vulnerable in more ways than she probably wanted to think about, but she was as proud and independent and prickly about it as she was fragile. His actions had punctured that pride and independence and he'd deeply offended her.

"My mistake."

Cade's terse words were soft, but his expression was as hard and unreadable as a rocky cliff face.

Colleen sensed that she'd surprised him, and she'd probably just made them adversaries, though it was the last thing she'd come here to do.

The fact was, Cade was too formidable for her. And though she'd come to him hat in hand for a favor, she couldn't let him think that her request entitled him to impose his will on her in other things and make a doormat of her.

She should have protested his invasion of her room last night and the fact that he'd taken her car key, but she'd let it go because her feelings about it confused her. What he'd just done with her rental car had been a clear wake-up call and made her realize she had to set a boundary, however belated. If she didn't, he'd walk all over her.

And if she let him do that, he might just go the whole way and decide that she was unnecessary to the children's upbringing. Though it was a risk to make him angry, it was a greater risk if he didn't respect her.

They stared at each other and Colleen suddenly felt panicked. She didn't know what to do now.

Cade glanced away briefly to open the passenger door of his car. ''We've got some decisions to make, Colleen.'' He looked at her. ''I overstepped with your car. I'll have it replaced.''

Colleen hesitated a moment more then stepped shakily forward to the car door. Now the prospect of being in a car again took her complete attention.

Dizzy fear whirled over her. Would it be like this forever? Cade had her seated in the car in moments and closed the door. She set aside her cane and hurried to get her seatbelt on so she could clasp her hands in her lap to conceal their tremors.

Cade got in then and started the car to pull out of the motel parking lot. Her terror spiked high but Cade's calm competence behind the wheel eased some of her fear of riding in a vehicle that shared the road with semi-trailer trucks.

By the time they reached the restaurant, some of her terror had calmed to simple tension and it made her feel better to be reminded that enduring her fear took some of the power from it.

After they'd ordered breakfast, Colleen silently battled the intense self-consciousness of sharing a private meal with Cade. She'd never been a clever, sparking conversationalist, and she felt even less clever and sparkling beneath the quiet scrutiny of his dark gaze.

"Why do you suppose your sister and my brother were married to each other for more than four years, but you and I are still strangers? Did you not care to come out to the ranch?"

Colleen glanced away to hide the flash of hurt. "M-maybe it's best to not look back." Her fingers fidgeted on the napkin-bundled silverware at her place.

She couldn't admit to him that she knew Sharon had frequently invited others to the ranch, but had rarely invited her. She'd been determined to ignore the hurt and not dwell on Sharon's reason. Besides, Colleen had gotten to see the kids often when Sharon came to visit her in San Antonio, so she'd let herself be satisfied with that and she'd never asked Sharon for more or hinted too strongly that she might have liked more.

But Cade apparently wasn't easily deflected when he wanted answers. "You think the ranch is too remote?"

Colleen glanced at him, then let her gaze stray, as if she was a little distracted by the activity in the restaurant.

"It's not really that remote," she said quietly. "The house is beautiful. And huge." Her gaze came back to his, sensing she should say more to assure him that she had no criticism of his home. "Built to raise big families in, I imagine. And maybe it needs to be that big because the land is so overwhelming. Doesn't it sort of minimize the shock of land size? If it was a small house, then going in and out every day might feel…odd."

Heat scorched her skin. Her lack of eloquence— her babbling answer—made her rush to make up for it. "Beau and Amy can be proud to grow up there. It's where their history is."

Cade's relentless scrutiny finally eased and she felt herself relax a little. Apparently he was satisfied. Or so she thought until he went on.

"Have you ever been on a horse or spent time on a working ranch?" he asked then, and she knew instantly that he was probing for something.

"No to all that. Not that it doesn't sound interesting," she added carefully. "My therapist suggested horseback riding, but I haven't looked into it yet."

"Why don't you stay on for a few days? Give Beau a chance to know you again and spend some time with Amy. A little time on horseback will strengthen you and we could drive out in one of the pickups and watch some of the work while you see the land.''

He paused as if he sensed her sudden reservations, and added with subtle skill, ''It'd be easier to take Beau and Amy out if you were along. They haven't seen much of the ranch or the work because I can't watch them every minute. The nanny we've got now doesn't really care for the big outdoors, and it's important for the kids to be exposed to their heritage from the ground up.''

The waitress delivered their food then and Colleen welcomed the interruption. She didn't know what to think of all this and she needed a moment to mull it over before she answered. He'd put it all in a way that she would naturally find irresistible, because he'd mentioned its importance to Beau and Amy.

That almost felt like a manipulation to her, but why would he do that? He'd never have to manipulate her into spending time with the children, so she took it as a signal of his approval of her involvement in their lives.

When the waitress finished setting their food in front of them and hurried away, Colleen's gaze caught on Cade's.

''I noticed you didn't really answer me, Colleen, about why we're still strangers and why you didn't come to the ranch much.''

She fumbled mentally for a way to deflect his curiosity. ''I thought I made it clear that it's sometimes not good to look back.'' It was a bold way to speak to Cade, but he didn't appear to take it adversely.

''Most of the time it's better to know the why of

things," he told her mildly, but with an undercurrent that let her know he meant to find out.

Perhaps she should tell him the why of things. If she told him the truth, it might discourage him from pressing her in the future for answers she didn't want to give.

Suddenly her appetite began to fade. As if he'd seen some indication of that in her tense expression, he relented. "I'll let you eat in peace." And then he turned his attention to cutting into the breakfast steak he'd ordered.

Colleen spread her napkin on her lap and started on the fluffy eggs, bacon and hash browns she'd ordered. The meal was perfect, and she was suddenly so ravenous that she ate most of her food before she finished the last of her coffee. It had been months since she'd eaten so much.

Cade talked her into sampling the cinnamon rolls he'd ordered for them and afterward, she felt stuffed. The huge meal had settled her nerves and she was beginning to feel drowsy.

"You look like you could use a nap," he remarked with a faint smile and Colleen glanced away.

Cade saw every little thing about her and he didn't hesitate to let her know it. He made her feel transparent, but he was also one of the few people who'd ever paid such close attention to her. She didn't know what to think about this or how she should handle it.

"I haven't been out of bed long enough to have a nap," she told him. It frustrated her to have so little stamina. "I'll be fine once I walk around."

"Give your body time," he told her. "You need to be coddled a little, get some exercise in the fresh air and sunshine, and eat lots of good food. You can get all that at the ranch.''

Colleen's gaze shot away from his. She was suddenly so restless and agitated that her drowsiness lapsed into rare bit of temper. "That's very kind of you, Mr. Chalmers, but I don't need to be coddled. And please don't feel sorry for me. You have nothing to make up for because I don't blame you for anything.''

She reached for her handbag, but when she reached for her cane, she managed to knock it off the edge of the booth seat and send it clattering to the floor. The waitress who'd been passing the booth stopped in her tracks to avoid tripping. She picked the cane up and handed it to Colleen with a smile.

Colleen's soft, "Thank you," was strangled and her face felt on fire. She took the cane, then slid to the edge of the booth seat and took special care to stand up as smoothly as possible. She couldn't look at Cade, who'd got to his feet much quicker. He tossed a couple of large bills to the table and Colleen was too agitated to argue that she could pay for her own meal.

The morning air was much hotter when they stepped out into the bright sun. Colleen was suddenly stricken with remorse for her choler and she could barely contain her upset until they were both in Cade's car and he'd started the engine. She couldn't look at him.

"I apologize. I'm not usually so cross. Or rude,'' she added, her mortification deepening by the second. She nearly jumped out of her skin when Cade touched her arm. Her gaze flew to his.

"How do I know that, Colleen? You offered to let yourself be evaluated, so consider staying at the ranch the next few days as part of that evaluation."

Now she saw the harshness in him. The implacability.

"Th-that's not possible."

His harsh expression went even harder and sent a breath of unease through her. The mildness between them that morning now seemed like a mirage. Cade Chalmers was not a man to trifle with and there was no sign of pity in him now.

"We're strangers, Colleen. There's only one sure cure for that. And you're the one who came to me for access to the kids."

Colleen stared, unable to argue with that, but she was suddenly afraid. When she'd offered to be evaluated, she'd only thought about it in the context of her relationship to the children and the evaluation of a professional. She'd never once considered that Cade would be that involved with her, or that he'd care to have more than a marginal knowledge of her outside her involvement with the children.

We're strangers, Colleen. There's only one sure cure for that.

Her impression—that he meant to know her and know her very well—was something she heard in the way he said the words more than in the words themselves. He'd made it sound like a mandate that required a familiarity with each other that would be separate from the children. And personal.

She'd become personal with few men. As she stared over at Cade and felt his strong will and the blunt power of his personality, it was impossible not to feel overwhelmed by him. Though women like her rarely had to deal with men like Cade Chalmers, she was being pressured into it now.

And that was the reason she felt overwhelmed by him and afraid of this. Because compelling, virile men like him were never attracted to plain women like her, though women like her were almost always in danger of losing their hearts to men like him. And inevitably they suffered the quiet agony of never having their feelings returned.

Colleen was the one who looked away first. She made herself think of Beau and Amy and tried to feel less threatened. But she was distracted by the drive back to the ranch. Again, Cade's competence behind the wheel was reassuring. He was alert, but calm. It helped that they met only three semis before they reached the ranch road and turned off.

"You're nervous in cars now, aren't you?"

It wasn't really a question, but Cade's remark was further proof that he was very perceptive. She thought she'd hid her tension well and she'd been sure he'd watched the highway the entire time and hadn't once looked at her.

Her stiff, "Yes," came out on a faint breath of defeat.

"Pretty hard to drive all that way by yourself, then. I'm sorry for that, Colleen."

The way his voice had dropped and gone rough touched her and made her emotional. She didn't dare look at him.

"I had to face it sometime," she told him, trying to sound philosophical about it.

They were both silent until they reached the house and got out to go inside.

Though Colleen had made clear her reluctance to stay on, Cade took her suitcase into the bedroom nearest the main part of the house. Beau's bedroom was next to hers on the same side. The nanny's bedroom was across the hall from hers, with Amy's bedroom next to that, and an empty bedroom next to Amy's. The door to the master suite, which was Cade's, was the last door on the hall and the room faced toward the patio as did Beau's and Colleen's.

Cade's office was in the other wing, he explained, along with a family room and a large playroom. There were two other guest rooms in that wing. Esmerelda lived with her husband elsewhere on the ranch.

With so many bedrooms, it was indeed a house to raise large families in, but the Chalmers family had never been large, though they entertained lots of overnight guests.

Colleen was disappointed that the nanny had taken the children to play at a nearby ranch. They wouldn't be back until lunch. Apparently, Cade hadn't expected this and she felt uneasy about the wait. She had enough anxieties about seeing Beau that she'd hoped to get it over with while she was still reasonably fresh and prepared to deal with whatever his reaction to her might be.

On top of which, she thought her presence might be awkward for Cade, that he might have other things to do besides keep her entertained. But she agreed to walk with him on a tour of the headquarters because

she could use the exercise and she thought it might
help pass the time. To his credit, Cade didn't give so
much as a hint that she might be keeping him from
something more important. Her biggest worry then
was that she'd wear out too soon.

"We'll see the kids at lunch, but after their naps,
we'll spend enough time for Beau to get to know
you again."

Colleen tried to move faster. Cade walked at her
pace and she worried that he'd be impatient with that.
But then he caught her elbow to slow her.

"I don't mind the pace, Colleen."

The warmth of his grip sent a flash of heat through
her, chased by a shivery sweetness that went deep
and quivered. She was in a situation that was so completely foreign to her that Chalmers Ranch might
have been an alternative universe.

In her world, she was invisible. Strangers did not
just take her arm. Even the medical people who were
now so familiar to her touched her only in a clinical,
necessary way.

But Cade Chalmers' long, hard fingers were
wrapped casually around her elbow as they walked.
He'd taken hold of her to slow her pace because he'd
sensed she was forcing herself to move more quickly
than she was comfortable with. But once she slowed,
he didn't let go of her.

After a few excruciatingly tense moments, she
forced herself to relax. But the peril in that was that
Cade's touch impacted her more deeply, sending the
sweetness through her in shimmering waves. She did
her best to concentrate on the tour and ask appropriate questions. They strolled along together for nearly

forty-five minutes before Cade circled back to the house.

Again, she was disrupted when he let go of her elbow and took her hand to place it in the crook of his arm. As if he knew her legs were now tiring swiftly, he casually slowed their pace even more and she glanced at him.

His profile was hard, but she sensed no impatience in him. She began to think that perhaps his rugged looks and natural gruffness gave an impression of harshness that looked stronger and more intimidating than he meant it to be.

Because behind his terseness and his forceful personality was a surprising gentleness. And that attracted her too much, so she looked away. The appeal of a tough, protective man who was also tender and gentle was strong for her. Too strong. And the steely strength of the arm that so easily supported her set off an earthquake of emotion and feminine excitement.

The biggest challenge was not recovering her health and regaining her closeness to the children or being allowed a place in their lives. Her biggest challenge would be to not fall in love with Cade Chalmers.

CHAPTER FOUR

BEAU and Amy didn't make it home for lunch and that angered Cade. More and more this past month, the kids, with or without their nanny, had spent a significant amount of time with Angela Danner. Angie'd taken them yesterday to play with her friend's kids, but he'd made it clear then that the kids would stay home the next few days.

He thought he'd made it clear to the nanny, too, but Connie was firmly under Angela's influence. He'd seen that for weeks, but he hadn't done much about it. Now he realized he should have taken a stand.

He'd dated Angela briefly a couple of years ago, but they weren't suited. Angela had been overindulged all her life by a doting daddy, and Cade had no patience with high-maintenance women who had to be the center of attention. His father had blazed that trail and his brother Craig had followed the same path.

Though Angela had declared years back that she planned to marry him, he'd never taken her seriously. He didn't intend to ever marry, and since he didn't, he'd narrowed his sexual focus to occasional no-strings dating, and never with local women, Angela in particular.

If he had time for Angela when she showed up, he saw her; if he didn't, he continued to work. He had a ranch to run and now a couple of kids to raise. As long as Angie didn't hinder any of that, he didn't mind her being around. At her worst, Angela was an entertaining pest. At her best, she was a neighbor being neighborly. Her attention had been good for the kids these past weeks and they seemed to like her.

But now he had suspicions about what had become of Colleen's letters and phone messages. Angela showed up here a lot and when she was around, she had the run of the place. It wouldn't necessarily surprise him if he found out Angela had done something with Colleen's letters and calls, but if she had, she'd gone miles over the line. And the nanny would be flirting with dismissal if she again allowed anyone's wishes to override his regarding the kids.

He'd have a talk with both women later. Now he and Colleen were having lunch in the eating area of the big kitchen. Esmerelda had left the room. Colleen looked exhausted and he felt a strong stir of guilt.

"Did I wear you out?"

Color touched her pale cheeks. "I don't have much stamina and I don't spend a lot of time outdoors these days. It's the fresh air, I think."

"I need to do bookwork this afternoon. You might as well use the time to rest."

Colleen's gaze came up to his, then shifted away. "I appreciate that. Unfortunately, naps are a fact of life."

Cade didn't comment and Colleen stifled the urge to repeat the phrase that had become a mantra: *But I'll get better*. Half the time, they felt like empty words. She was frustrated by her slow recovery.

Though she'd come a long way, she still had so far to go that she despaired of ever recovering her strength.

But she didn't want to be pitied. She watched Cade a moment. His rugged face was solemn and harsh. She again got the impression that his harsh expression was merely the way the man's face looked, that he might not be half so harsh in his manner or thinking. He'd been very gentle with her. Domineering and driven to have his way, but gentle. She didn't want him to think she meant to take advantage of it.

She lifted her napkin off her lap and blotted her mouth. The movement drew his attention and his dark gaze met hers.

"I don't want to be a burden, Mr. Chalmers."

"Cade."

The gruff correction made her wonder if he'd heard the rest of what she'd said.

"I don't want to be a burden or a bother to you, but I have limitations. I'd rather you speak up if any of them cause...inconvenience."

A rare smile curved his hard mouth and lightened his stern expression. "I rarely keep my thoughts to myself."

"Nevertheless," she persisted, but the sudden glitter in his eyes silenced her.

"You're terrified of pity, aren't you? But maybe you don't understand the difference between pity and compassion. Or friendship." He paused. "What if I was the one with the cane? How would you like it if I mistook your kindness—or your good manners—for pity?"

Colleen shook her head. "The fact is, I should be more recovered by now, I feel like a malingerer."

"So you feel guilty because you can't do handstands yet. Kindness embarrasses you because you think you don't deserve it. Dr. Amado says your recovery is remarkable, considering your injuries."

Colleen glanced away, restless. "Dr. Amado is very generous. You make me sound more brave and noble than I am. Please don't do that."

Cade leaned back in his chair. "I'll think what I please, Colleen."

That alarmed her even more and her gaze flew to his. Whatever she thought about seeing a gentle side to him, she was still starkly aware of the harshness in his personality. Especially the harshness in his judgments. "Please don't idealize anything where I'm concerned. I can't live up to an ideal."

Now he did smile and her heart skittered with a feminine delight that confused what she was trying to communicate.

"Do I look like a man given to idealizing worthless females?"

"No, but—"

"Let it go, Colleen." Now his smile eased away and his rugged face hardened a little. "I'm satisfied by what I see. And I'll think what I want about it."

Colleen couldn't tear her gaze from the solemnity in Cade's. He was saying something to her that she couldn't quite grasp. Something deeper than his words. It was there in the way the room stayed silent, there in the laser intensity in his dark eyes and his almost hypnotic power to hold her gaze.

He'd made some judgment about her, one so significant that he'd somehow altered the course of her life. He'd invaded her somehow, approved something he saw, and now he was zeroing in. She wasn't certain she could handle the kind of closeness that implied. What could this mean? What did she hope it meant?

It was amazing how hard it was to force her gaze to break contact with his. She was imagining things. There was no hidden message in what he'd said or in his long, steady scrutiny. It was her appalling lack of experience with men that made her think there was. Cade's intensity meant nothing special or significant. He was an intense man. That's all this was. He would be this way with any woman. With anyone.

Which underscored the emotional peril of being in close contact with him. Colleen couldn't help being attracted to Cade.

And therein lay the peril. She was terrified of misreading him, for mistaking his kindnesses for something they weren't. God help her, she couldn't take it if she found out she was a pathetic, love-starved female so desperate for love that she fell for a man who could never possibly love her, then mooned after him the rest of her days.

Terrified she had the potential to be just such a woman, she laid her napkin on the table and reached for her cane. She was overtired. Surely that's what all these attraction and alarm and doomsday feelings were about.

"I think I'll go rest now," she told him, embarrassed to sound so flustered. "You will call me, won't you, when the children come home?"

"Yes."

Cade's voice was gruff and she didn't dare look at him to see if he meant the harsh way he'd said the word, as if she'd displeased him somehow. It would devastate her if she saw evidence that he'd sensed her foolish feelings. Better to not look at him, better to act as if it was easy to not look at him, better to give the impression that he didn't interest her in any way beyond the children.

She managed to defy the weak legs made temporarily weaker by her long walk that morning and got to her feet. Then she made a respectable exit, though she felt Cade's gaze follow her every step of the way.

"What letters?" Angela flashed him a smile and forced her light brows into an appropriate look of confusion.

Angela Danner was beautiful. Her shoulder-length blond hair was wild with natural waves, her body was centerfold perfect, and her face was breathtaking: flawless skin, large blue eyes, classic features, and lush lips that Cade suspected were not naturally that lush, but had stealthily evolved to look it these past couple of years.

Angela was stunning, but she was also lying. He'd always had misgivings about her, but now they were beginning to take on shape and definition. She'd intercepted Colleen's letters and phone messages, probably taken them from the tray on his desk where Esmerelda routinely left them. And that made him furious.

His expression must have turned a little fierce because Angela suddenly looked flustered. Cade's brain flashed a picture of Colleen's face when she was flustered, and his mind did a lightning replay of her other expressions as well as the shadows of pain and mystery in her robin-shell-blue eyes.

He was staring at the incredible, breath-stealing beauty before him, but his brain was suddenly fixated on another kind of beauty, Colleen's beauty. The beauty of a shy woman with character, deep feeling, and as much inner steel as she had physical limitations. A woman with more humility than her share who might be too intimidated by him to lie to his face, and yet had so much pride she was prickly about it. And that made her Angela's complete opposite.

"Colleen James' letters and phone messages, Ang." He was careful to keep his voice soft and noncommittal. "If you have an explanation, you need to make it."

Cade could almost see the mental scramble Angela made. She studied his face as if searching for a clue to his feelings—and for the clue to how to get around them. He saw it the moment she decided to be candid with him.

But in her case, it was a decision to be bold and confident. Traits that, in the context of Angela's character, he considered arrogant; as if stealing Colleen's letters and messages were righteous acts she'd defend to the death because her selfish motives were lofty ones.

Angela gave a dismissive wave of her manicured hand. "Colleen James caused enough trouble and heartache for the Chalmers. She waited until Craig died to make contact with you because he wouldn't speak to her while he was alive. She probably figured to catch you in a weak moment.''

''For what purpose?''

Angela gave him a scoffing look. ''Neither one of the James' girls ever had anything. Sharon had her looks and figured out how to use them. I suppose Colleen decided she'd try to exploit her tie to Beau and Amy. She's a cripple now, but she had the nerve to show up here yesterday, looking all pale and pitiful.'' Angie's lip curled. ''So how crippled is she, really?''

Now Angela approached him and ran her long nail tips lightly along his jaw. Her voice went husky.

''And you're a soft touch, Cade. You couldn't resist poor little plain Colleen any more than you could Beau and Amy. Even a timid little mouse like Colleen James could figure that out.''

She smiled and reached up to wrap her arms around his neck, oblivious to the quiet fury building in his chest. Boldly, she pressed her fabulous body against him as if she was confident she had him in her sensual power.

''Send her away, Cade. I hear she has a huge settlement offer from the trucking company, so she can live without your money. The kids will be better off without her. Their lives are here now, you're the one they need. And,'' she added, giving him a smile she must have thought looked sincere, ''I love them, too.''

Cade didn't move. He stared down into Angela's beautiful face, both transfixed and repelled. He sensed what was coming before she spoke the words in her honeyed Southern belle drawl.

"Daddy asked me the other day why I didn't just go the rest of the way and move in over here. But I told him I was holding out for a ring and a date." Her expression turned artfully shy and she dropped her gaze to his shirtfront to walk her fingers coyly up his buttons.

Her barely concealed smile told him she considered a marriage proposal from him her due. It amazed him that he'd let her go on this long, that he hadn't thrown her out the moment she'd made her confession. But this was enough.

"Leave."

His terse order startled a laugh out of her and her bright head came up. She stared at him strangely, as if she thought she hadn't heard right.

"What?"

"Go home to daddy."

"Cade?"

"Tell him you'll never find a ring and a date on this side of the fence."

Angela pushed back from him slightly, and her perfect face paled. "You don't mean that," she scoffed cautiously, then made a sound that was half nerves, half laugh. "Cade?"

Cade took hold of the hands on his shirtfront and eased her away from him. He released her but she stood frozen, absently shaking her head.

"You don't mean that. You can't."

"I mean exactly that. Don't test me."

The next backward step Angela took was under her own power. She seemed to fumble for something to say. "Wh-what about Beau and Amy?"

"Not your worry."

Angie pressed her fingers to her lips as she absorbed the shock. But then she collected herself. The confident—arrogant—female she'd been her whole life instantly reappeared. She lowered her hand, clenched it into a small fist, and gave him a glittering look.

"I'll let today go by, Cade. I don't know what's happened exactly, but I *do* know you don't mean this. Craig's death upset you even more deeply than any of us imagined. You just need time."

Cade watched with false calm as she automatically shifted the blame away from her own actions. It outraged him that she'd again brought Craig into this, but he concealed it and said nothing.

Which turned out to more effectively prompt her angry exit from his office and his house than if he'd ushered her out. He followed at a slower pace, then watched from the front door she'd flung open and left standing wide. Angela Danner got into her car and roared off in an explosion of gravel and dust.

The small travel alarm woke Colleen from her nap. She'd slept for over two hours and felt surprisingly refreshed until she realized she wasn't nearly as refreshed as she was excited. Beau and Amy should be home by now, and the thought of seeing them again caused her as much anxiety as hope.

Cade was satisfied that Colleen wasn't responsible for Beau's reaction to her yesterday. He was certain things would go well now, but Colleen could take nothing for granted. She made her way from the bedroom to the central part of the house. Cade was just stepping into the living room from the entry hall when she came in and he saw her.

"Feeling better?" His dark gaze moved over her as if seeking evidence for himself.

"Yes, thank you," she said quietly. "Are the children home yet?"

"In the playroom. I was about to see if you were awake." He crossed to her and together they went to the playroom.

Beau was running a dump truck on the carpet and Amy sat on the floor nearby, closely examining the face of the cloth doll she clutched in her tiny hands. Both children looked up, but Amy was the only one to respond favorably. She set her doll aside and crawled directly to Cade, who leaned down to pick her up. Amy's attention was riveted on Colleen.

Colleen smiled at the child, but her gaze strayed briefly to Beau, who had quit playing to stare, but stayed where he was. Cade ignored Beau's lack of reaction and directed Colleen to the sofa on the opposite side of the room. They both sat down, Cade still holding Amy.

Amy pointed to Colleen and chattered a few words to Cade that made no sense to Colleen. Cade answered as if he'd understood perfectly.

"This is your Aunt Colleen. Tell her 'howdy.'"

"Howee." Amy grinned, pleased with herself. "Howee!"

"Howdy to you," Colleen said, smiling though her voice was choked. Since the accident, she'd become embarrassingly emotional and it took everything she had to keep her smile in place.

Beau was still staring and aloof, and Amy was too

restless to sit still. She pushed away from Cade and carefully slid down his chest to his lap, then down his legs to the floor. She went directly for Colleen's cane, which Cade casually reached for and removed from harm's way.

Thwarted, Amy stopped crawling and sat down as if to think about it before she crawled off to her toys. Beau hadn't moved and was still staring solemnly at Colleen until Cade called him over. Beau picked up his truck and stood, then walked their way with obvious reluctance. He climbed onto the sofa next to Cade and sat back.

"Hey, bud, say hello to your Aunt Colleen."

Beau's attention was on the dump truck in his lap. He didn't look up and he didn't speak. Thankfully, Cade didn't press. Instead he asked the boy what he'd done at Angela's house that day.

Colleen listened to Beau list the things they'd done that day, but he spoke in a quiet monotone and she felt sick. Something was even more wrong now than yesterday. Cade had been certain the problem was solved, the misunderstanding straightened out. Even Colleen hadn't believed things with Beau would be *this* bad. But there was no way to put a pleasant face on things now, no way to interpret Beau's reaction to her as anything but complete rejection.

Would Cade change his mind about her involvement in the children's lives? Though it tore at her heart, she had to admit that he would be compelled to reconsider. As much as she wanted to be with the children, it was completely possible that her involvement might not be what was best for them. Especially not for Beau.

Somehow, she endured Beau's somber silence. She was only able to do so because Amy was so clearly fascinated with her. Once Amy had piled several of her toys in Colleen's lap, she climbed onto the sofa and into Colleen's arms to play.

Through it all, Beau kept a wary distance, watching his baby sister closely, as if at any moment he might need to rush over to rescue her.

Supper was even worse. While Amy sat in her high chair, Colleen fed her a selection of baby food, happy to divide her attention between her meal and the child's. But again, Beau warily watched her every move and Colleen saw plainly the worry in the child's vigilant gaze. Not even a couple of gentle questions to the boy got more out of him than a "yes" or "no" answer. It was only marginally less upsetting that Beau was just as brief with his Uncle Cade.

In spite of the fact that Colleen was eager to spend every moment she could with the children, she couldn't help her relief when after supper the nanny came to whisk them away for their baths. She and Cade moved out to the patio to enjoy the warm evening air. Colleen spoke the moment they sat down at the heavy wood bench just outside the kitchen.

"I think I should go back to San Antonio for now. Tonight. Beau feels too pressured." Now she looked over at Cade's unsmiling face. "And if you've changed your mind about my involvement with them, I…"

Her breath came out in a disheartened rush and she looked away so he couldn't see the hot tears that burned her eyes and stung her nose.

"I haven't changed my mind, Colleen."

His rough voice was so calm, so solemn, so certain. Somehow instead of being a comfort or a reassurance, his words only added to the misery she felt. She made herself look at him.

"Maybe you should," she got out. "The boy is clearly upset by my presence. He was terrified I'd do something to hurt Amy, I could see it in his eyes."

"It was irrational for him to be upset."

Cade's easy dismissal of Beau's feelings made her angry. "I don't care if it was irrational or not, he was upset. Clearly he can't help how he feels." Now she got to her feet, using the cane much more because she was restless and distraught and her legs felt even weaker.

Somehow, she had to be on her feet to emphasize her decision because there was something about standing while Cade sat that made her feel less dominated. "I want to go back to San Antonio tonight. I won't put him through another moment of upset."

"Give the boy time."

"We did give him time, and all it's done is make things worse. I don't want him pushed." Now she fidgeted with the head of the cane, struggling to hide the pain. "You promised you'd get me another rental car. I want it now, please."

She dared a glance in his direction to let him know she expected him to keep his promise. Cade leaned back on the bench and studied her flushed face. "You aren't in any shape to drive."

"Then I'll call someone to pick me up or I can pay one of your cowhands to drive me," she told him with quiet fierceness. "I'll walk if I have to, but the boy's been through too much. I won't be the cause of another second of upset for him. A-and I want him to know I'm gone *before* your nanny puts him to bed. I don't want him to have nightmares because of me.''

''What about your upset?'' Cade's voice was still calm and the question made her emotional.

''I'm an adult, not a three-year-old child who's just lost both his mother and father,'' she told him, unable to keep her voice from rising with frustration. Why didn't Cade understand her reason for wanting to spare Beau? He was looking at her as if he didn't get it.

''I-if anyone has to be upset, it should be me, and I'll be glad to do it if it gives the boy peace and some sense that he and his sister are safe.''

Cade was watching her in the same frustratingly calm, solemn way but his dark gaze was now razor sharp. ''He needs you, Colleen.''

Now the tears surged so hard and so strong that her vision blurred. She turned away suddenly, lost her balance a little, but pushed away Cade's hand when he was at her side instantly to steady her.

She gritted her teeth against letting a single tear escape and got out, ''He needs *you*, Cade Chalmers. H-he needs a safe, peaceful home where he's adored and cared for...''

She literally couldn't finish her declaration because the effort to keep her roiling emotions back was too difficult to do and still speak. Instead, she turned shakily to walk past him and go inside the house.

Cade caught her arms and refused to let go. She

tipped her chin down and gritted her teeth. "Damn it, let me pass. I want to go home."

The small profanity was completely out of character for her, and Cade must have been surprised by it, too, because she felt his grip tighten fractionally.

His gruff voice was curt. "On one condition. That I drive you now, but you plan to come back when I come to San Antonio to pick you up in a couple of days."

The small sob slipped out and she nearly choked keeping a second one back. She tried a retort to distract him from what he surely must have heard. "I c-counted two. Two conditions."

Cade came right back with, "Not me. I counted one for you and one for me."

"I want to go home. Now," she whispered, feeling more and more as if she was caught in a nightmare that had no end. "I can't pro-omise the other."

He did the most remarkable thing then. She had no warning and no time to prepare. She couldn't believe it was happening when suddenly Cade pulled her gently against his big, hard body and wrapped her in his arms with a careful fierceness that amounted to the first true comfort she'd felt in years.

Her shaking body instantly melted into his and his heat seemed to weld her against him. Her arms came around his lean middle. She dimly heard her cane clatter to the patio stones, but suddenly the only thought she was capable of was to wonder how on earth she could manage to stay in Cade Chalmers' hard, strong, *gentle* arms forever.

CHAPTER FIVE

THE ride to San Antonio seemed to last forever. Colleen was so exhausted she could barely keep her eyes open, but she was too on edge to allow herself to relax. Cade's big Suburban was heavy and high profile, and though it felt much safer to travel in than her rental car, it was still not equal to the size and power and weight of the semi-trailer trucks it shared the highways with.

When they got to her apartment building, she managed to walk into the building and make it to her unit under her own power, but she'd clearly overexerted and she'd pay for it with a restless night and a hurting day tomorrow.

Cade carried her overnight case and he unlocked her door to escort her in. He walked through the living room to the hall and the bathroom, flipping on lights for her, then carried her case into the bedroom she indicated.

He'd been wonderful to her and she was as flattered by his attention as she was disturbed and confused by it. She didn't understand any of this.

"You got a bed in your other bedroom?"

Colleen didn't realize the significance of Cade's question and answered. "Yes. Sharon and the kids used that room when they came to town."

Cade opened the door to the second bedroom and Colleen winced. That room was now a kind of shrine to Sharon and the children. It was the larger of her two bedrooms because when Sharon had brought the kids to visit, they'd needed a room large enough for all three of them. There was a double bed, a baby bed and a crib for an infant.

Colleen had never wanted Sharon to stay in motels when she brought the kids to San Antonio. And the last month of Sharon's life, she and the kids had lived here. Though they'd all been upset about the separation, it had been heaven having the people she loved most living with her.

Colleen sat down on one of the living room armchairs. She could see Cade from where she sat. He'd reached in to turn on the light in the bedroom, but instead of going in, he'd stood in the doorway staring. Then he reached back in, switched off the light, and backed into the hall to close the door softly.

He'd understood the significance of that room and his solemn manner conveyed silent respect for what it was. He walked back into the living room and she got wearily to her feet to walk him to the door so she could lock up.

"Thank you for bringing me home."

Cade's dark gaze swept over her and the memory of being held so tightly against him sent a flash of pleasure through her. He stopped little more than two feet away and gave her an implacable look.

"I won't leave you alone. Your sofa will do fine."

It took her a moment to comprehend his declaration. "You can't stay here."

She caught her breath at her outburst then rushed to make up for how rude and ungrateful she'd sounded. "I d-didn't mean to sound...rude. Are you tired?"

Surely that's why he meant to stay. It was a four-hour round trip for him. He was an early riser, so the trip back might make the day especially long for him. No one knew the peril and fatiguing stress of long car rides better than she did. She should have considered that he might be too tired to drive home.

Cade's steady look was unnerving. "I'm not tired, Colleen. You shouldn't be alone tonight."

Colleen gave her head a small shake. "I'm fine." She even tried a faint smile to back it up. His dark gaze sharpened.

"And that's a lie." The grim pronouncement dealt her a new shock and she felt herself sway with it. "You lied to me yesterday, too."

"No...when?"

His sharp gaze never wavered. "Seems to be every time you put the words 'I'm' and 'fine' together. Because you're anything but fine when you say it."

It wasn't that he disapproved of that kind of lie, that was plain from the gentle timbre of his voice and the soft darkness in his eyes. But he clearly meant to make some point about it and he would be immovable on the subject. Colleen felt a small aftershock.

"That's my problem, Mr. Chalmers. I'm not your worry."

"*Used to be* your problem. And people worry when they want."

Baffled by this, Colleen glanced away, frustrated and a little scared by the way he seemed determined to take over. Because of Beau, they might never have a reason to see each other again after tonight. This sudden invasion of her life was flattering, but it would hurt more in the long run if she allowed it now.

She couldn't let herself have too big a taste of this. Far better to not know precisely how wonderful it could be to be with a man who seemed to care what happened to her. Not when she had no hope of keeping him around. That hug before they'd left the ranch was already unforgettable.

Colleen tried to be careful how she deflected him. She didn't want to insult him for being kind, however macho and domineering he was about it. She couldn't look at him as she said the words.

"I know you m-mean well, Mr. Chalmers." She cringed at how stiff that sounded and tried to moderate it. "I think that beneath all your macho stuff you're a very kind and gentle and generous man."

Her lips had moved quicker than her weary brain. *Macho stuff?* Oh, God! Humiliation strangled her, and her gaze flew to his.

Cade reached up and pulled off his Stetson to upend it on the lamp table at the end of the sofa. Colleen's horrified gaze tracked the move before it sped back to his face. He gave her a slow smile.

"My *macho stuff* will do just fine on your sofa."

Oh, God! But then the stress of the past couple of days caught up to her in a new way and, triggered by her mortification, a wild little giggle tumbled out. Colleen jerked up a hand to stifle it, but the giggling fit wasn't easily stifled.

"I didn't mean to say it that way," she got out, defeated by another burst of giggles, "hon-honest."

She struggled, helpless with mirth as she swayed and her legs went dangerously weak. "I can't even remember what I was trying to say when that came out."

She made another try for sobriety and tried to fix a serious expression on her smiling mouth as she bravely looked over into his stern face, but it was impossible. "I meant no—" another giggle slipped out "—disrespect—oh, God, I'm so sorry!"

But Cade was chuckling over it now and the change in him was dramatic. He was so handsome.

"You are so handsome when you smile. Your laugh is so—" The shocking words continued to flow fluently before Colleen caught herself, appalled. Her face felt on fire but she couldn't get the wide, foolish grin off her face. "S-so sorry again. I don't even know what I'm saying anymore."

And because she didn't, the giggles vanished and her mortification turned to tears. Suddenly she found herself swept up into Cade's strong arms. He'd managed to catch her cane when she'd reflexively grabbed for his wide shoulders.

His dark gaze was gentle as he stared down into her wet-lashed eyes. "You're quite a comedian tonight, Colleen, but you need some sleep."

Her head was still whirling from the sudden movement of being picked up, but it felt so wonderful to be held again, to have Cade hold her, and now he was carrying her to the hall and her bedroom. Her emotions seesawed wildly between giggles and tears, but she was terrified she'd cry. Sadness and longing smothered the giggles and her heart was suddenly drowning in misery. As Cade carried her into her room, she was incapable of keeping the words back.

"Please don't."

He stopped beside the bed, but he didn't put her on her feet. "Don't what?"

"Don't take care of me. Please don't."

Now he went still and his dark eyes were grim as he stared down into hers. "How you gonna make me stop, Colleen?"

"I know you mean well."

Cade bent down and set her gently on the edge of the mattress. He straightened, braced her cane against the night table next to the bed, and gave her a stern look. "You *know* nothing of the kind."

"Yes, I do. Amy and Beau love you very much. If you weren't good and kind..."

She choked off the words. Telling Cade why she thought he meant well—and mentioning the children's love for him as proof—was an agonizing reminder that little Beau now mistrusted her and was afraid of her. Following the logic she'd used to determine Cade's character, that meant her own character must be truly awful.

She was startled when Cade's big hand settled warmly on her shoulder. "Best thing for you tonight is to get some sleep. If you need something in the night, I'll be close by. If you wake up and can't go back to sleep, I'll sit up with you."

Colleen brought her hands to her face and pressed her palms against her hot cheeks. She squeezed her eyes closed against the sting of tears and shook her head. "Please, Cade, don't. I can't h-handle it."

Cade gripped her thin shoulder and gave it a small

shake. His voice was stern and certain. "Beau's gonna come around. When he does, he's gonna need you."

"I can't count on that. I can't even hope for it."

The room stayed silent a long time. Colleen couldn't look up at Cade because she was too close to tears. His hand didn't move and eventually, she felt the heaviness in his silence and was startled to realize she sensed anger. She heard it distinctly in his deep voice.

"I'm wondering how the hell you made it this far, Colleen James."

The growl in his low voice made her pull her hands from her cheeks and look up at him. His expression was stony. He was so tough-looking and his next words to her were just as tough.

"Reach down deep into whatever it is that made you live through that wreck, and take hold of something you can use. Because I've got no patience with a woman who'd quit on a kid, especially a kid she claims to love."

Cade crouched down in front of her and reached for her sneakered foot. He briskly peeled open the Velcro tabs, pulled off the shoe and tossed it aside, then reached for her other foot to give that shoe the same brisk treatment.

Colleen stared, chastened, encouraged and shamefully emotional. Cade's hard dark gaze came back up to hers and she felt the concussion of the sudden contact. He was still crouched before her and he'd braced a big fist on the mattress beside her knee.

"Speak up if you want to use the bathroom. I reckon I can get you into your nightclothes and into bed if you need help with that." Now the faintest of smiles curved his harsh mouth. "I'm takin' care of kids now, so I've had the practice."

His tough talk was over and now he was blunt and practical. Colleen couldn't help that she put out a hand to touch his shoulder. It had been spontaneous and out of character for her, but she'd been overwhelmed with the need to do so. He'd just done her enormous good, but she couldn't think of a word to say to him that wouldn't sound foolish and sentimental to his macho ears.

"I can handle things from here, thank you," she said quietly. "You can use the other bedroom. Or I can sleep in there and you can have my bed."

Cade straightened then and gently caught the hand she'd rested on his shoulder. "The sofa's fine. Or the floor. I sleep out in a bedroll on the ground more often than you think."

She wasn't comfortable with that, but she was too exhausted now to argue. "Then there's extra bedding in the hall closet. Towels, too, if you want to shower."

Cade nodded and released her hand. "Much obliged. Good night."

"Good night." Colleen watched him leave the room. Later, she lay in her bed, her heart pounding with worry and gratitude and what felt a whole lot like love.

What happened that next day made Colleen wonder if she was dreaming. She'd slept surprisingly well, considering the upset and exertion of the past two days.

Cade had gone out while she'd showered and he'd brought back a huge carry-out breakfast. He'd mildly scolded her about the lack of food in her refrigerator and cupboards, so after breakfast, he gently bullied her into going with him to a grocery store.

He left just before noon. Colleen sat in her living room in the aftermath of his gentle juggernaut. She'd enjoyed spending the morning with him. They'd done nothing spectacular, but he was pleasant to be with in spite of his stern manner.

And the small things he'd done—he'd untangled the knotted drapery cord in the traverse rod over the sliding door to her small patio, and he'd used tools from his Suburban to fix the drip in her kitchen faucet—might have been small things to anyone else, but not to her.

Something in her had relaxed and opened up. Cade made her feel cared for and she'd needed to feel that. Despite what she'd told him yesterday, she'd needed to have some gallant someone sweep into her life and give her something she'd never seemed able to get for herself. There were only so many positive affirmations you could repeat to yourself without someone in your life to validate them.

Hope burned bright again. Things with Beau would work out, her life would work out. She'd passed a new milestone in her recovery. Thanks to Cade. Thanks so very much to Cade. No wonder the children adored him.

That afternoon, she pushed herself at her therapy session and asked for harder, more frequent exercises. Her therapist commented on her improved attitude, which made Colleen feel vaguely ashamed to have let depression hinder her determination these past months.

On the return home, she got off the bus two blocks before her usual stop to lengthen the walk to her apartment. She quickly learned that the concrete was punishing, but that the ground along the sidewalk made walking easier.

She was exhausted by the time she let herself into her apartment, but she regarded the exhaustion as a good sign. She'd earned it today. Next week, she might be less exhausted and shaky, and the week after, she might be even stronger. Now she was consumed with pushing herself, pressing as hard as she was able toward a full recovery.

Colleen took a long shower, fixed a sandwich, then fell asleep watching the early news. The buzzer from the lobby woke her later and she got up stiffly to go to the intercom to find out who it was. Cade's voice startled her.

"I'd like to see you, Colleen."

Surprise and pleasure sent excitement through her and she buzzed him in the lobby door. She was dressed in a pair of jeans and a T-shirt, and ran frantic fingers through her hair, grateful she'd combed in a bit of mousse after her shower to tame it. She heard Cade's heavy bootstep in the hall and opened the door.

Cade looked formal somehow, though he wasn't dressed formally. He wore jeans and a white shirt, but he'd donned a black suit jacket and a string tie with a silver concha. He took off his black Stetson and waited for her official invitation to come in.

Now his formality sent a quiver of fear over her.

She'd been foolish to think he'd come all the way to San Antonio so soon for any reason but a serious one. And for her, a serious reason to justify a long drive could only mean that something was wrong with the children.

"Please come in." She could hardly wait until he walked in and closed the door. "Are Beau and Amy all right?"

"The kids are fine."

Relief eased her anxiety but Cade was so solemn that new worries sprang to mind. He stood rigidly before her and she was suddenly self-conscious.

"Please sit down. Can I get you something to drink?"

"Nothing for me, thanks." But he made no move to choose a place to sit. He nodded past her toward the sliding door to the small patio. "The evening's warm, but nice. Mind if we sit outside?"

She got the impression that Cade was uneasy, which was surprising. But he was a man accustomed to the outdoors, so perhaps he would be more comfortable outside in the evening air.

"If you'd be more comfortable outsi—"

His quick glance cut her off. Had she offended him by putting it that way or was he merely surprised that she'd guessed he was uncomfortable?

Colleen led the way to the sliding glass door, but Cade reached past her to open it. Once they were through and he eased the door closed, they both sat down on the slatted bench.

Cade leaned forward. His forearms rested on his hard thighs while he rotated the Stetson in his hands.

Such big hands, rough and scarred and dark from the sun.

Colleen sat back and secretly stared at his profile while he looked out over the shadowy lawn between her building and the next one. His ongoing silence made her fidget. There was a tension about him that was mystifying.

She was immediately worried that he'd changed his mind about her. That maybe he'd decided Beau might never get over his feelings. If that was so, then perhaps Cade now felt regret for the things he'd said to her last night, that he'd got her hopes up only to have to dash them tonight. He might even be reluctant to hurt her when he knew how much she loved the children.

"If it's bad news, I'd rather you just said it," she said quietly, then held her breath.

Cade glanced over at her. His dark eyes moved over her face then dropped lower before he abruptly looked away.

"Not bad news," he said, though the way he said it suggested he wasn't convinced.

So Colleen couldn't truly relax. And she couldn't bring herself to prompt him to go on. It was clear he was brooding over something. When he did speak, his voice was low and calm, but carried the same thread of tension his last words had.

"Have you got a special man in your life, someone you want to...make plans with?"

It was an astonishing question. It amazed her that *anyone* would ask her that. Obviously she was the last woman who would ever have a special man.

Anyone could see that. She'd never had a date, never even been kissed. And that was before the accident.

Other than pride, there was no reason for her to not be honest with him, no reason to pretend to him that she was anything other than she was.

Her voice was quiet. "Let's just say I'm not the first female who comes to mind when most men plan their Saturday nights. I've never...dated."

Now he gave her his complete attention, sitting back a little to look at her. The cranky whorl of his dark brows and his terse, "Why the hell not?" made her heart swell with secret pleasure. Blunt as it was, what he'd just said ranked as the sweetest thing any man had ever said to her.

"You have eyes, Mr. Chalmers," she replied with soft candor.

Now those dark eyes gave her face such an intense inspection that she was taken aback. But then his gaze dropped to her breasts and took a long, slow inventory of her whole body. She'd never had a man look at her like that and her instinct was to cover herself. But then his gaze came up to hers and pierced deep.

"I'd like to see more weight on you, longer hair, but you look fine to me. Damned fine."

Colleen stared, so shocked she felt the world tremble and spin. It was a moment before she remembered to breathe. He was so convincing.

Now he looked away, eased forward again to rest his forearms on his thighs and stared across the shadowy lawn. "This'll be a bolt out of a blue sky, but there's something I want you to think about."

He'd changed the subject on her and she mentally raced to keep up.

"The kids need a mama and a daddy who love them, two parents who can settle their lives and raise them right."

Colleen immediately jumped to the most natural conclusion for her. Cade planned to marry. Why that hurt was no mystery to a woman who'd just been given a sweet compliment by a man who'd genuinely seemed to mean it.

Because, just her luck, that man's single days would naturally be at a premium. And, just her luck, the only man who'd ever said she looked "damned fine" to him, would never think to actually choose her for anything so sacred and wonderful as marriage. She stared at his big hands now as he toyed with the crown crease on his Stetson.

"I think I'm about to shock you, Colleen."

He rotated the Stetson a couple of times, as if he was giving them both a few moments to prepare. He'd already shocked her, so she couldn't imagine what he could possibly say next that would be a bigger shock. When he spoke, his voice was low and rough, almost a rasp.

"I planned to never marry. I don't believe in love, not the hearts and flowers kind. Craig had the kids, the family had heirs, so there was no reason to bother with women beyond dating to get certain needs met. Never saw marriage as worth the hellish bother the last few Chalmers' marriages turned out to be."

The Stetson made another few turns in his hands and Colleen tried to calm the restless beat of her heart. Cade's attitude toward marriage was a surprise.

His reference to his sex life and how he'd gone about getting "certain needs" met was very personal. Too personal to be telling to her. He didn't appear comfortable confiding that, but she sensed his determination to do so however he felt about it. Or however she felt about it.

"I changed my mind about marriage today," he said, making a new start. "The kids need stability. They need a regular life. You love them like I do, and I think we can give them that regular life."

Colleen sensed what was coming then, *knew* it, but couldn't believe it. Cade was right, he was shocking her. She put out a trembling hand and gripped the armrest of the bench as he went on with gruff relentlessness.

"Beau will come around. Amy takes to you. They could have a mama and a daddy again, only more grown up and settled ones than they had before. Maybe it'll make up for the harm to them, maybe what they lost won't hurt how they grow up from here on."

Colleen began to feel light-headed. Cade leaned back and looked at her pale face.

"I think we should marry, Colleen."

Her heart gave a huge leap. Cade still had his iron composure, but she felt faint. She couldn't move, couldn't speak. Her pulse began to pound heavily. This had to be a dream.

If anyone had asked her what she thought was the most outrageously impossible thing that might ever happen to her, she wouldn't have been able to come up with anything more outrageously impossible than

Cade Chalmers declaring to her *I think we should marry.*

They barely knew each other, so there was no love here. And because they barely knew each other, how could they possibly consider marriage?

Cade set his Stetson aside then and got up to ease down to a crouch in front of her. He took her cold hands, and they all but disappeared when his big fingers closed around them.

"Too blunt?" His stern mouth settled into a gentle curve. "You okay?"

Colleen made an effort to speak. "I...never expected—"

His grip tightened warmly. "The kids need a whole family, Colleen, not just an uncle who can't be with them every minute and an aunt who comes around sometimes."

"We barely know each other. And Beau..." She hated to put Beau's rejection of her into words. And Cade knew what was going on, so there was no need to spell it out.

"I'm satisfied with what I know about you, Colleen. I can see your character, and I think a lot of you. The biggest thing for me was what you were willing to do to be with the kids, but then you were willing to just walk away if that's what was best for them. You couldn't care less about me beyond getting access to those kids."

How could that possibly be enough for him? And he was already wrong about her. She *did* care about him. Too much, though she didn't know him any better than he thought he knew her. He went on while she fumbled for a way to confess that.

"I'm damned tired of women who see me as a meal ticket. Or a trophy. But in your case, if I wasn't the doorway to the kids, you probably wouldn't give me the time of day. And that speaks of priorities I agree with and admire. The kids come first."

Colleen looked down at his big hands, unable to speak yet, but uneasy with the guilt of not admitting her feelings for him. He was wrong, so so wrong. She would have given him the time of day whenever he'd wanted it.

But, oh, God, how could she turn this down? To have a marriage proposal from a man you were as strongly attracted to as she was to Cade—especially when she suspected she was already falling in love with him—was a sweet fantasy come true. And she'd be able to raise Beau and Amy herself. This was the chance of a lifetime for a woman who'd had no realistic hope of ever being married or having a family. But aside from the kids, there was no love here, at least not on his part. Not yet.

Could she live with it if he didn't love her? How would that affect Beau and Amy? What if he could never love her? Would he still want to be married to her? Or would their marriage end up being the nightmare her own parents' had been? The children would suffer tremendously then, as she and Sharon had.

The silence stretched out now. She should correct Cade's impression of her, she should politely decline his proposal. But Colleen found she couldn't bring herself to turn him down, or to even strongly discourage the idea of starting a life with him and the children in a loveless marriage.

She had to force herself to look him in the eye

and prayed her feelings for him wouldn't show despite what she had to say.

"We don't have...love. I know we both love the children, but all we have is maybe friendship."

"Friendship's a good start, Colleen." Now his mouth settled into a stern line and his expression went utterly serious.

"I told you I don't believe in the red hearts and flowers kind of love and I haven't changed my mind about that. So I'd consider love a liability. I can offer you caring, respect and commitment. Responsibility, friendship. Desire, affection. More reliable things than love."

It was an impressive list. But how on earth did you have those things if you didn't have love? Wasn't love the spark that made the rest possible? Wasn't real love defined by those very things? And yet those things were separate from love in Cade's mind. And why was that?

"So you think those things aren't a part of love?"

"Rarely." Now his stern face carried a hint of fierceness that was a little unsettling. "My daddy was crazy in love with a woman who wasn't worth a minute of his life. Craig was crazy over Sharon and we both know the hell they had for a marriage. I've seen others. Too many."

Colleen felt compelled to disagree with Cade's bleak prejudice against love. "I never believed that what Craig and Sharon had was what love is supposed to be. At least it didn't seem...healthy," she told him quietly, but a deep flush edged his cheekbones and she got a stark glimpse of resistance in him.

"I won't let history repeat, Colleen. I'm offering you a common sense marriage. But the focus is on the kids and raising them in a stable home. Nothing can get in the way of that."

His fingers tightened gently on hers and she looked down at his big hands, troubled. He was giving her a very stern edict, and because he was so implacable, it was another shock. For all his love for Beau and Amy and his gentleness with her, it was hard to believe he objected so strongly to love, that he'd hardened his heart to what he called the "red hearts and flowers" kind. And considered it a liability.

Given her own history as a sad witness to her parents' marriage and to Sharon's, she should have felt the same way. Instead, those bitter marriages had given her a clear picture of what love was and what it wasn't. She'd always been certain she'd recognize the real thing if good fortune ever smiled on her, so the fact that Cade wouldn't consider love was a huge disappointment.

Would he ever change his mind? It was an unhappy truth that she was probably the last woman on earth that a man might change his mind for. She wasn't a very persuasive person.

What should she do now? What could she do? The sensible thing would be to turn him down now, whatever happened with Beau.

But she already knew she might never have a better offer. Her heart began to tremble under the weight of the choice.

CHAPTER SIX

CADE suddenly felt regret for the way he'd proposed to Colleen. He could tell his declaration about love worried her. And maybe it had hurt her feelings.

Women like Colleen were naive and because they were so inexperienced, they were full of romantic notions and hopes. In her case, she'd been through a lot of hard times and she was the kind of woman who deserved to have good things come her way.

He meant to give her good things. Number one was that she'd be close to the kids and get to help raise them. He'd see to it she felt cared for, that she'd never want for any material thing. He'd be a gentle, considerate husband and he'd give her the best.

He'd be so good to her that she wouldn't notice if he never said all the pretty words. She'd be content with everything else because he'd make sure of it. She'd have a small piece of his heart—hell, she did already because he liked her—but not so big a piece that she could use it to make a fool of him. No woman would ever do that. He'd never give any female that power, not even Colleen.

This talk was fair warning, so he shouldn't regret it. He'd meant to get them started the way he planned for things between them to go. The only way he'd allow *his* marriage to go: a common sense marriage with clear boundaries.

Colleen looked up at him then and he was again

struck by the sadness and mystery in her eyes. And now the anxiety.

"You said you wanted me to think about this," she told him. "I will, but things are still not...resolved with Beau."

This was what had made him trust her from the first, that she kept putting the kids' feelings ahead of her own.

"And," she began again, then stopped. Now the sad mystery in her pretty eyes seemed stronger suddenly, and her gaze wavered a little. He caught a glimmer of what was coming. "And, I have lots of...limits."

"Like what?" He'd known she would bring those up, he could have bet money. This was also part of the reason he'd changed his mind about marriage. Because Colleen always seemed determined to tell him everything she thought was fair for him to know.

"I can't keep up with active children right now. It'll take time before I'm fully recovered, and I can't tell you precisely when that will be. There's a possibility I won't ever recover one hundred percent. I can't do complicated math yet, I'm more emotional, and so far, I can't even tie my shoes. Those things especially, I can't guarantee. And I have...scars." Her gaze shied slightly from his before she forced it back. "Lots of those."

He could tell from the anxiety in her eyes that she was deeply worried about those things, that it was important to her that she confess it all. As if a list like that might make him change his mind.

He should have been offended that she thought him that shallow, but he was touched that she was honest enough to risk it. An odd warmth bloomed in his chest and he gave her hands a squeeze.

"So, we'll have a nanny, you won't have to work round-up, and you can use my math software. We'll all wear boots or Velcro shoes. And I've got scars, Colleen. Lots."

The brisk recitation coaxed a small smile from her, as he'd hoped. He'd left one thing out, and he tried for a worried look so exaggerated she'd have to know it was fake.

"But emotion?" He put a bit of emphasis on the word. Then he saw the worry that shot through her solemn gaze and realized he had to be careful. He'd meant to lighten things up, but maybe he wasn't good at it. Why he suddenly wanted to become good at it didn't bear close scrutiny

"I reckon my macho stuff can handle emotion, Colleen," he told her then chuckled to show her that her "macho stuff" remark still tickled him. "I've got a few emotions of my own."

He enjoyed the color that surged into her cheeks as she understood he was gently teasing her, that he meant to make her smile. He felt her relax, but she wasn't done with the subject.

"I have more of a...temper now. And I get weepy. More than before."

Cade took that seriously. She was still worried, so he was blunt. "As long as you don't use tears to manipulate me or the kids, and you don't let your temper loose on them, we won't have trouble, Colleen. Anything else?"

She'd got the message about manipulation because

he saw the reaction in her eyes. He could also see she was tiring.

"Thank you," she said softly. "I'll think about all this, but we have to wait for Beau."

Cade straightened, his firm grip on her hands bringing her to her feet. He reached for her cane and waited until she had it firmly in hand before he released her. He walked her back inside, locked the patio door, then took her elbow to be sure she walked with him all the way to the hall door.

She deserved to know right away that their marriage would have a physical side. She was surely a virgin, and since he planned for them to marry as soon as possible, she needed to be eased into the sexual side of their relationship. He should start now.

Colleen stopped at the door and the fine tension between them shot high when Cade turned to her and slid a hand around her waist. She'd expected him to briefly tell her goodbye and leave. Instead, he turned fully toward her and eased his other hand around her waist. Colleen glanced up and saw the determined look he gave her.

"I don't want you to worry about Beau. What you need to think about is marrying me."

Cade pulled her closer and she put up a hand, hesitated when she couldn't decide where to put it—or that she should touch him at all—and stared warily up at his stern face. She could suddenly see what was coming, and her knees went spongy. Her heart went wild. She tried to move back, but Cade tightened his grip to prevent it.

"We're marrying for the kids," he told her, "but I don't plan for either of us to live celibate."

And then he was leaning down and his lips settled firmly on hers. Colleen couldn't help that she gasped and reflexively drew back, but Cade didn't let her get far.

His lips were warm and sure and expert. Colleen felt a moment of self-consciousness before Cade swept it away. Later, she wouldn't remember losing her cane when her shaking hands came up and she was suddenly hanging on to him for dear life. Her legs gave way almost immediately, but Cade was prepared.

His kiss—her very first—was a seductive tutorial, and when his tongue eased between her soft, pleasure-crushed lips, she nearly fainted with sensation. Her aching body was suddenly light and tingling, and the bold, sensual invasion of her mouth sent a heavy, electrifying heat to every feminine part of her.

Too soon the devouring pressure of Cade's mouth began to ease. She was helpless, so drugged with pleasure that she was insensible. By the time he slowly drew back, she was gripping his hard forearms. She couldn't have spoken a word to save her life. It was as if he'd short-circuited her brain and now nothing worked.

She struggled to make her legs support her. When she was finally able to stand without his support, her stupor lifted enough for her to feel fiery heat in her face.

Cade must think her a sexual pushover, so inept and inexperienced that one kiss had turned her into a quivering ninny. A *gasping*, quivering ninny. She'd made desperate little sounds that shocked and shamed her now.

A more sophisticated woman wouldn't have been so easily overwhelmed. And a more sophisticated woman might have known far better than she did how to reduce a man like Cade to the same shaking, rubber-kneed zombie he'd so easily made of her.

She dared a look up into his rugged face and saw a fierceness that startled her until she saw the satisfied curve of his stern mouth.

His voice was gruff. "Think about that, too, Colleen."

Spoken by a man of experience who was confident of his sexuality and understood its precise impact on the woman he'd chosen to focus it on. Now she read the male arrogance in him. She should have been offended, but after a kiss like that, her only thought was that he'd earned that arrogance. She'd never dreamed a kiss could be that shattering, that incredible.

He smiled down at her. "Sleep well, baby. I'll bring the kids over tomorrow."

Baby. The endearment spoken in his gravelly drawl was possessive. Blatantly possessive.

Cade picked up her cane and put it in her trembling hand. Colleen struggled to appear composed though her face felt like a scorched mask.

"Good night." And then he was gone, closing her door solidly, leaving her with her heart in an uproar.

I don't believe in the red hearts and flowers kind of love... I'd consider love a liability...

Colleen thought she'd understood what he'd meant when he'd declared those things, but remembering them now was deeply confusing. How much different would his kiss have been if he *did* believe in love? If he loved her?

Perhaps the real question was, could she have survived it?

That next day, Colleen tried to prepare herself for Cade's visit. He was bringing the children, but he hadn't said when.

He arrived with them in late morning. And he'd accomplished something of a miracle. Beau walked in shyly, but when he looked at Colleen, she didn't see wariness.

Cade's big hand rested on the boy's head as a gentle guide and subtle restraint. The moment he lifted his hand, Beau set down the large diaper bag he carried and sprinted across the living room to the hall and the bedroom he'd shared with his mother and baby sister. The familiarity of that gave Colleen hope.

Her anxious gaze shot to Cade's. He was still carrying Amy and he had a second diaper bag slung over his shoulder. Going by that, Colleen had to conclude that she expected this to be a long visit.

"Don't worry. I told you Beau would be all right."

As if all Cade Chalmers had to do was snap his fingers and the planets would realign. She might believe he could if he had accomplished a miracle with Beau. Her impulse was to follow the boy to the bedroom, but she was leery of pressuring him. There was nothing he couldn't see in that room, so she let him explore it alone.

Amy had one small arm around Cade's neck and

the fingers of her other hand in her mouth. She managed a wet smile around them when Colleen smiled at her. Amy appeared delighted with her attention. To prove it, she pulled her damp fingers from her mouth and gave a little laugh.

"Howee!"

Colleen couldn't help the giggle of surprise that tumbled out. She put out her hand to the child and caught the baby's damp fingers. "Howdy, sweet girl."

Suddenly Amy was reaching for her with both hands. Colleen felt instant frustration. There was no way she could safely take the child into her arms and hold her while she was standing.

Cade intervened with a quick, "Sit down somewhere."

Colleen turned and went to the sofa, sitting on the middle cushion. She set her cane aside and reached for Amy as Cade handed her over.

The tiny girl grabbed on to her and put her arms around Colleen's neck. Colleen wrapped the child in a tight hug, not caring that Amy's little knees and sandal toes dug painfully into the tops of her thighs. Her tears were pure joy and she slipped up a hand to wipe them away so Amy wouldn't notice them when she pulled back from the hug.

But Amy didn't end the hug. Instead, she shifted, digging in with her knees and toes as she made herself comfortable against Colleen.

The smell of baby shampoo and powder was intoxicating, and Colleen pressed several kisses in Amy's wispy dark hair. She managed a teary look up at Cade, who'd seen everything.

"Thank you."

Cade took note of the fact that Amy's little knees and sandals rested squarely on Colleen's legs.

"Is she hurting you?" he asked gruffly.

Colleen's breathless, "I don't care, I'll move her in a minute," made him sit down next to her to gently shift Amy's legs in a way that put her knees on either side of Colleen's left thigh. Which also slid Amy lower against her. Amy lifted her head to look over at Cade before she settled against Colleen again, content, her head resting on Colleen's chest, her fingers back in her mouth.

Colleen forgot to be shy with Cade about the kiss last night. As she held Amy, she studied his so-harsh face. This man would never mean her harm, *could* never mean her harm.

He might not believe in love, but if his effort to reunite her with Beau and Amy wasn't loving, then she didn't understand love at all.

Cade eased back against the sofa. He sat so close that they touched from shoulder to knee. "Beau and I had a talk yesterday and more today at breakfast. It's a long, twisted-up story, but the short of it is that someone said the wrong thing to him. It's straightened out now. Once he sees that room and things came back to him, he'll come around."

Colleen watched Cade's calm face as he spoke and felt her affection for him grow. She knew he meant for them to do the best they could for the children, but it seemed to her that his marriage proposal was above and beyond what was necessary to do that.

He was sacrificing himself for the children, offering marriage to a woman he didn't love, passing up the opportunity to meet the woman who might change his mind. Resolving problems to clear the way so he could make a marriage pledge to a woman who was far less than he should have been able to demand in a wife.

"Whatever happens with Beau, I won't hold you to your proposal if you change your mind," she said quietly. She had to offer him a way out. He was too wonderful to not be given a second chance to rethink what he truly wanted.

"My mind's made up."

His terse answer made her glance down and tighten her arms around Amy. He was so certain. But then, he was a man who was probably never tortured by indecision. Colleen envied that. She returned her attention to Amy.

It felt so wonderful to feel the warm weight of this child in her arms, to have Amy's small fist cling to her blouse. *Heaven.* But a Heaven with a small cloud of discontent. There were almost no sounds from the bedroom. What was Beau doing?

As if Cade had the same thought, he got to his feet. "Too quiet." He strode to the hall, then stopped at the doorway of Sharon's old room. He looked on a moment, then said to Beau, "Why don't you bring some of those things out here," before he started back to the living room.

Cade had no more than sat down beside her again before Beau came out of the bedroom, carefully leading a pull-toy mother duck and her babies by its heavy string. The quacking sound of the ducks made Amy sit up and zero in on her brother's prize.

The moment Amy saw what it was, she pushed

away from Colleen and slid down her legs to the edge of the sofa, then down to the floor to crawl off at high speed to get to the ducks. Beau saw her coming and led the ducks in a wide circle that bypassed his sister briefly before he turned and led them within her easy reach.

Amy had stopped crawling and was sitting up, crowing over the ducks that stopped and went silent when Beau stopped walking. He crouched down and handed his little sister the string and Colleen felt a huge swell of emotion.

"Aunt Colleen byed me these at a place one time. Don't eat the string."

And of course, the first thing Amy did with the prize string was to put it in her mouth. Beau grabbed her little fist and pulled it away from her mouth, but the minute he let go of her hand, she tried it again.

Colleen watched, so moved by the sweet sight of the two children together, that she had to battle the blur of tears.

"Here, Amy," Beau said, then set about trying to distract his sister from putting the string in her mouth. He pulled the ducks forward and stopped them by Amy's feet. It was obvious someone had taught Beau to use one toy to distract his sister from less wise play pursuits, and Colleen watched with interest to see what the baby would do.

Amy took the bait, leaning forward to grab on to one of the baby ducks and gleefully drag them all closer. But the minute she singled out the last baby duck, she picked it up, pulling all the ducks along, to put the little duck in her mouth.

Beau sent Cade an exasperated glance. "Uncle Cade—Amy won't stop slobbering on the toys!"

Cade was already chuckling, and the warm, masculine sound wrapped around her heart. Cade's arm dropped over Colleen's shoulder and tightened to bring her snugly against his side.

"Let her go, son. We'll dry 'em off later."

Beau had been looking at Cade, but his gaze shifted to Colleen and fixed solemnly on her. Colleen held her breath and tried a small smile.

"There's a teething toy in the crib, Beau," she dared gently. "It's okay to give it to Amy, but you might want to rinse it off in the bathroom sink first."

Beau instantly got up and ran to the bedroom. In seconds, he crossed the hall to the bathroom and there was a hard thump. Colleen smiled. The thump was the wooden step stool Beau needed to use to reach the sink.

She called out an automatic, "Be careful of the hot water," then felt a quiver go over her. How many times had she cautioned Beau about that in the short month he'd lived here? Sentiment roared up and her eyes stung with it.

Sharon had been alive then. Despite her separation from Craig, nothing in their lives had been irrevocable. They'd all been healthy and whole and close. So close. Now everything had changed. No one was whole anymore, none of them. Even Cade had been wounded by it all, especially by Craig's untimely death. The easy closeness of before was also gone. But perhaps about to come back... *Please God.*

Beau came running out of the bathroom. "You still gots my tub toys!" And along with the teething toy, he clutched a rubber dinosaur under his arm, his face bright and smiling. He came directly to Colleen, climbed on the sofa then stood on his knees beside her, completely forgetting to give his sister the teething toy.

"Uncle Cade! This is my Rocky. He takes baths with me." Beau dropped the teething toy to put Rocky the dinosaur's big belly between his small hands. The loud squawk he got out of the creature when he squeezed its belly made him laugh. "He's dried out now, so he makes a big noise."

Amy heard the noise, too, abandoned the ducks and came to the sofa to investigate. She used fists full of Colleen's jeans to pull herself to her feet and tried to climb to Colleen's lap. Colleen couldn't reach for her quickly enough to suit her, so Amy let out an irritated squawk that sounded so much like Rocky's that they all laughed. Cade reached over to snatch Amy and settle her gently on his lap.

Beau started to bounce on the sofa cushion and now he stared at Colleen. She tried her best to keep the tears back, but oh, God, she so wanted him to remember the happy times with her, she so wanted things to be reconciled between them.

"Uncle Cade says you missed me a bunch," he said, and his high little voice sounded untroubled and natural. "Does your legs hurt?"

Colleen could barely get out the soft, "Sometimes," around the massive lump in her throat. "Getting better though."

"I'm glad," he said, and it sounded genuine. "You know my mommy died, didn't you?"

Colleen had even more trouble now. It was obvious that the boy was confused about the accident and how she'd been involved. On the other hand, it might have been the only question he knew how to ask to open the subject. "Yes, Beau. I know. It was very sad."

Beau suddenly sat down beside her, still holding Rocky between his small hands as he looked the toy over. Colleen took a huge chance and put her arm around the boy. She hadn't been able to stop herself. To her profound relief, Beau automatically leaned in against her, completely accepting the half embrace.

Beau turned his head and looked up at her while she struggled to keep a smile in place and not cry. "Uncle Cade says you're gonna come live with us so we can all be a family. Can you bring Rocky and the ducks?"

"Of course I can." Colleen couldn't help herself then and reached to put her other arm around the boy. Beau wiggled and got up on his knees before she could so he could hug her around the neck.

Colleen almost drowned trying to keep back tears of gratitude and relief. Just as Cade had promised, he'd solved things with Beau. And a miracle of that magnitude, accomplished so quickly and this completely, made it impossible for Colleen to even consider denying Cade Chalmers anything he might name in return.

By the time Cade took them all out for lunch and they'd come back to the apartment, they had two very tired children on their hands. Colleen was just as tired, but she tried to weather it. Together, they put the kids down for their naps, Beau in the double bed and Amy in the baby bed. The crib was too small for her now, so Cade disassembled it and carried it over to Colleen's storage unit in another building of the apartment complex.

By the time Cade returned, the kids were fast asleep and Colleen was dozing off sitting up at one end of the sofa. Cade came in silently, but when he put his hand on her shoulder to try to lay her down, she woke up fully and declined. She reached for her cane and stood.

"Would you like some iced tea? Lemonade? I can start some coffee if you'd prefer that."

Colleen was still emotional about the reconciliation with Beau. The need to do something to show Cade her gratitude was overwhelming. Offering him something to drink was such a small thing, but it was all she could think of.

"Why don't you rest for a few minutes?" he said, still not choosing a place to sit. "I haven't read the newspaper yet and I can wake you in an hour."

Colleen shook her head. "I haven't done enough today to earn a nap."

"Sleep heals, Colleen."

"I know," she said softly. "I can sleep after you all go home."

"Was planning to take you home with us later," he said, and Colleen was surprised. "Hadn't got around to mentioning it yet, but had it in mind."

"I have a therapy session in the morning." Now the encumbrance of the frequent sessions made her feel even more impatient with her slow recovery.

"Why don't you call your therapist and ask about

riding horses? Might be just as good as what you're doing now. Probably better.''

Colleen's face flushed. ''I have a confession to make,'' she said, figuring she might as well tell him now.

Cade's dark eyes glimmered with interest. ''Bet I can make a guess.''

Because she dreaded confessing her secret to a man who was surely an excellent horseman, she gave him a small smile. ''All right. Let's hear it.''

Cade didn't hesitate. ''You're afraid of horses. Either fell off when you were a kid, which I doubt because Sharon had never been around horses before, either, or now that your body's been through so much, you're afraid to take a fall and make it hurt worse.''

Colleen glanced away, not really surprised that he'd guessed it precisely. She looked like the kind of woman who'd be afraid of her own shadow, so it was probably a simple enough conclusion to come to.

Nevertheless, so many other men seemed obtuse. Her own father had been oblivious to the fears and pains of others, particularly his wife's and children's. And she'd never seen much evidence that Cade's brother Craig was nearly as perceptive as he was. That thought wasn't a criticism of Craig in particular. It was merely the most common observation of a woman whom others rarely bothered to analyze because they never truly looked.

Cade paid attention to everything. She felt as relieved about that as she was on guard against it.

''Yes. You're exactly right. I feel a bit fragile.''

"We'll be careful. I can't guarantee you'd never fall off or get thrown off sometime, but while you're still healing and new to it, I'd do everything possible to make sure you have safe rides. I've got a twenty-year-old gelding that the kids around the ranch ride bareback all the time. Hasn't bucked anyone off—or tried to—for years."

Colleen nodded. "I'll take your word for that, and I'll hold you to the safe rides for now."

"Why not ask the therapist? After that, we need to talk over a few things. Unless you change your mind about that nap by then."

Colleen had to drag her gaze away from Cade. Every word he said to her was pleasant and easy. And she found his vigilance over her well-being profoundly comforting. He made her feel cared for, as if she had great value despite her current limitations. Colleen couldn't help but be seduced by that.

Which made her wary. She mumbled something inarticulate to him about calling her therapist before she made an escape to find the phone number.

CHAPTER SEVEN

COLLEEN phoned the therapist and got her advice, then rescheduled her appointment for later in the week.

Cade was sitting at the kitchen table, glancing through the newspaper when she finished. She got an iced tea for herself and set a second glass for Cade within his easy reach.

As she chose a spot to lean back against the counter opposite the table from him, he asked, "Still fighting that nap?"

"I might have a small one before they wake up. I've been sitting too long, I need to stand awhile."

Cade refolded the paper and set it aside. He thanked her for the tea and had a sip before he said, "There's something we need to get out of the way."

Colleen heard his serious tone and put her glass on the counter to give Cade her complete attention. The look on his face sent a breath of anxiety through her.

He was brisk and direct. "We'll have to do a prenuptial agreement."

She knew prenuptial agreements were the done thing these days for celebrities and the rich, but she'd not really approved of them. To her, they cast doubt on the success the prospective bride and groom expected of their union.

Besides, she hadn't given him an official answer

on his marriage proposal. On the other hand, the strongest reason she'd given for hesitating was Beau. Now that Cade had solved that, he might consider her acceptance a foregone conclusion. Even so, she couldn't bring herself to remind him that she hadn't formally agreed to marry him. Yet.

"Is a prenuptial agreement necessary?"

Cade's rugged expression turned more remote, and she sensed something about his manner that made her uneasy. "If things between us don't go well, I need to protect Chalmers' financial interests for Beau and Amy."

Colleen was immediately alert to what he'd left out. "You don't...anticipate that you and I might..."

She hesitated, wishing she hadn't jumped into her question so quickly, because she suddenly realized the emotional peril of what she wanted to ask. She gave it another try because she'd said too much now to reconsider her wording. And she needed him to answer this. After all, this was the man who'd told her last night that he didn't plan for either of them to remain celibate, though she wasn't about to remind him of that now.

"You don't anticipate that we might have children of our own?"

Cade leaned back and studied her flushed face. "Hadn't truly thought about it. Don't have strong feelings either way. You want more kids?"

The heat in her face went higher. "I couldn't risk a pregnancy now, but...yes. If we marry, I'd want to have more children. They'd have equal parts with Beau and Amy in Chalmers' interests, wouldn't they?"

"Any children we have together would. What the prenuptial will address is divorce and what the alimony settlement to you would be if that happens."

Colleen instantly said, "I don't like..." before she stopped herself again. His reason for a prenuptial had rattled her. "If we marry, I don't like to consider divorce an option. It feels like...bad—"

She cut herself off, frustrated with her lack of eloquence. "Not bad luck. I mean jinx. I don't want to jinx the marriage by starting it with plans for divorce."

"Jinx or no, I want Chalmers' interests protected before we say 'I do.' We both need to know the limits."

And from the harshness on his face, she knew he was immovable on this subject, too.

"If we divorce in the first two years," he went on, "you get no alimony. For each year we stay married after that, your one-time alimony settlement will increase, starting with the second anniversary of the wedding. There'll be a year-by-year alimony amount written in the paper, which increases each year until it tops out after Amy's eighteenth birthday."

The "top" figure Cade named then jolted her. "It won't go up from there, no matter how many more years we stay together."

Colleen could barely breathe. Cade's "top" amount was such a shocking number—and surprisingly generous—but the worst of that shock had come from the cold-blooded way he'd spoken.

This was the tough Texas businessman who had money and power and knew how to wield it, protect it and make it multiply. She hadn't given this side of Cade much thought because it wasn't important to her beyond the fact that he worked hard for a living.

She'd understood him as a rugged, no-nonsense rancher who loved his niece and nephew. A tough, virile, gentle man who would make a strong, caring husband.

But on the subject of money and divorce, he seemed ruthless. There was an undercurrent beneath all this that was both coldly unemotional and flash-fire volatile. She heard it clearly in his next words.

"I won't let any woman threaten Chalmers' assets, Colleen. Not even you. If we go our separate ways, I don't want a court fuss. And once you have your money, you won't get a penny more."

The implacability she'd sensed in him before was now brutally stark. It was a warning that this man, if he chose, could run over her and crush her into the dust if she threatened his fortune or livelihood.

But he could also crush her in other ways that were more threatening to her and much more important. The memory of her parents' marriage was suddenly sharp. She didn't care about Cade's money or his material assets, but there was something else that was as important to her as Cade's money was to him. Now that he'd solved the problem with Beau, maybe it was time to bring it up.

"Could I have something in the agreement?"

The ruthlessness in Cade's expression eased by only a fraction, but it was enough to encourage her to speak.

"I don't care what you name for divorce settlements. As long as you don't plan for our marriage to be some kind of marathon ordeal.''

''What?''

''You're saying that the longer I stay married to you, the more money you'll give me in a divorce. If you turn out to be a rotten husband, you might not care to make an effort to improve if you think you can pay me for the time I endured.''

She saw the shock in his dark gaze and the ruthlessness in his hard face eased. A grim smile slanted his mouth and he gave a humorless chuckle. ''That's a suspicious and cynical take on it, Colleen. Wouldn't have thought that of you.''

But, remarkably, he seemed more open to her now, as if they'd reached some sort of consensus on reality.

''I made you promises last night about the kind of marriage I was offering you. I give you my word of honor on those.'' Now he brought them back to her request. ''You want something in the prenup. What is it?''

Cade had just handed her the opening she'd been struggling to find. ''Last night you listed caring, respect, commitment, responsibility, friendship, affection and desire. I know love wasn't on your list. But one you left out is something that's very important to me, and important to the children.''

His expression hardened fractionally, but she could tell he was curious.

The terror she felt suddenly made her head swim. She moved shakily to the table to sit down. It took her a moment to collect her thoughts.

''I don't mean to offend you.'' Now she looked

over at him and he was so solemn that she almost lost her nerve. But then she thought of the children and made herself go on.

"My father was probably never faithful to my mother. When she got sick, he thought she was faking to get his attention back on her. Then his infidelities became blatant."

She stopped as the memories sharpened and overwhelmed her. It was another agonizing few moments before she could dredge up the courage to make her demand.

"I know men cheat," she said quietly. "I couldn't stop you from doing that, I know. What I don't want is to know that you're doing it. I don't want to know if there are other women. If I find out, or the children find out, or anyone we know or socialize with finds out, then I'll...divorce you."

Cade was more grim than she'd ever seen, his expression so closed to her that she couldn't guess what he was thinking. She went on quietly.

"I'd like it put in the agreement that if we divorce because of infidelity, that I get primary custody of Beau and Amy and any children of ours. That you'll support them and me with a good house and child support until they finish all their schooling, even college. They can visit you often, but they will live with me."

Cade didn't hesitate. "The kids belong on Chalmers Ranch."

Colleen battled the sharp sting of disappointment. She struggled to stay calm. "Then you refuse?"

"If I couldn't be faithful to you, we wouldn't marry."

It was an impressive declaration and very believable, but it cost him nothing to say it. It was the easy way out because lots of men made promises they didn't keep. It took her a moment to comprehend what he said next.

"But you can have that in the prenup. Put in whatever penalties you want, short of mayhem, if it makes you feel safe. I'll sign."

Now his harsh face was relaxed again, solemn but with no trace of anger, no hint of resentment. And his dark eyes were kind, with none of the sharpness or fire she'd seen earlier. It was over and she'd got what she wanted.

A massive wave of relief and exhaustion rolled over her and she wilted. She braced an elbow on the table to press her palm to her forehead, partly to hold up her head, partly to make the room stop spinning. And a headache thumped hard enough to make her realize she either had to take something for it or go lie down for a while. Cade wasn't finished with the subject, however.

"I'll give you what you want, but I'd like an explanation of what you meant by blatant."

Somehow she'd known he'd ask her that, so she lifted her head and looked over at him. "It's a very ugly story, Cade."

His gaze was steady and intense. "I've seen ugly before. I might even tell you about it sometime."

There it was again, that glimmer of cold emotion and flash-fire temper. Colleen sensed then that if he ever told her about it, she'd have the key to his reason for seeing love as a liability.

It took her several moments to steel her emotions

so she could answer him. She didn't want to break down. Her instinct was to try to speak as unemotionally as Cade might. But she was weary now and this discussion about infidelity had stirred up more painful memories than she normally allowed herself to think about.

And maybe because she held so many back, it was dangerous to bring them up. Like chiseling a notch in a dam to release some of the pressure, but betting the whole thing wouldn't collapse. The last thing she wanted was to break down and have Cade think she was manipulating him or making a play for sympathy. He'd given her a very strong warning about that.

She started carefully. "As I said, my father was probably never faithful to my mother. He resented it when she got sick. He accused her of faking it to get his attention. So one afternoon, he brought one of his women home. He made our mother get out of bed and cook a big meal for them. Sharon and I had to help with most of it, because Mama could barely stand."

Colleen couldn't look at Cade now. She braced both elbows on the table and briefly combed her trembling fingers into her short hair, agitated and restless. Her voice was painfully hoarse.

"Then we all had to sit at the table and eat with them while he flirted with his woman. We weren't allowed to speak."

Suddenly, it was too much. If Cade hadn't heard enough to understand, then he never would.

"Pretty extreme, I know," she finished quietly. "I doubt you'd be cruel or that obvious, but it's devastating to a child when one parent does something that…dishonorable…to the other parent.''

She finished by looking over at him solemnly to say, ''Beau and Amy will probably grow up believing you hung the moon, so…'' She let her voice trail away. He could fill in the blanks there. He was so still. His tanned face had a ruddy flush and he looked stunned.

Colleen glanced away, suddenly so weary she could barely focus. ''I really need to lie down now, hope you don't mind.''

She'd rushed that last out because her head was hot and full of tears she wouldn't release. She fumbled for her cane, but Cade was suddenly at her side, bending down, lifting her off the chair into his arms. The movement made her head swim and she clung weakly to him as he turned and started out of the kitchen.

He strode into the hall, then to her bedroom. He took her directly to the bed and laid her down gently before he straightened and looked down at her. ''It's a little cool in here. You need a blanket?''

She was grateful that he was practical now. If he'd said something sympathetic, she would have burst into tears. It amazed her that he'd sensed not only that, but that she didn't want to break down in front of him. But she saw the worry in his eyes and her impulse was to reassure him that she was all right.

Colleen gave him a tired smile. ''There's one on the chair.''

Cade turned away and got the blanket. He efficiently shook the folds out, then dropped it gently over her.

"Thank you."

"Anything I can get you, anything I can do?"

There was another question behind that one, and Colleen answered it. "I'm really all right, Cade. Honest. Just tired."

His dark eyes searched her face as if to assure himself before she saw his rugged expression ease.

The memory of his kiss last night seemed to materialize in the air between them and Colleen felt heat creep into her cheeks. She watched him, unable to keep from tracing every detail of his face, unable to keep from trying to discern what his thoughts were now.

His voice was low and dark. "You haven't given me your answer, Colleen."

Her gaze shied from his. "I know "

"Marriage will solve things."

"Some things."

"We'll solve the rest in time." He reached down to touch her cheek and her senses spiked high at the soft contact. "Sleep now, don't worry about the time. I'll take care of the kids."

When he straightened and his calloused finger wasn't stroking her cheek, the world seemed to dim a bit. And then he was gone, closing the door softly behind him.

Colleen lay quietly and endured the ache of her tired body as she waited for fatigue to take her.

Cade's proposal was the opportunity of a lifetime for a woman like her. It could also be the biggest mistake of her life.

Could he really never love her? Every kind thing he'd done for her was evidence that he was a loving man, so his declaration about love mystified her. Perhaps she was the one who didn't understand love. She'd had so little of it herself that perhaps her notions about what it was and what it wasn't were too idealistic.

But as she lay there waiting for sleep to come, she could no longer pretend to herself that she was falling in love with Cade. The truth was, she'd already fallen in love with him completely, and now she had to face the consequences of that love, whatever those might be.

Given that and the fact that Cade wanted to marry her, which would be the mistake? Accepting his proposal...or turning it down?

In the end, Colleen couldn't help herself. She'd never been particularly adventurous, but after she'd rested and joined Cade and the children, the sight of them all together was so precious to her that she knew she'd risk anything to be a part of that.

What Cade had offered her was the chance to belong somewhere in a young family, to have a meaningful life with hope and energy and healing for them all. With children to care for and love, and a husband who could make her life more than she could ever make it by herself. And already had.

They got to Chalmers Ranch after dark that evening. Both children, already dressed in their sleepers, had fallen asleep in their car seats in the back seat of the Suburban. Cade pulled the big vehicle to a stop at the end of the front walk. Colleen got out on her side before he could come around to help her, so he gently unbuckled little Amy from her seat and gathered her limp, sleeping body in his arms to carry her to the house.

Colleen managed to get ahead of him and open the door before she went back out to the Suburban to wait with Beau in case he woke up. Cade was outside moments later and got the sleeping boy.

While Colleen lingered with the children, first in one room then in the next, Cade brought her things and the kids' into the big house, efficiently depositing everything in their respective rooms before he joined Colleen, who was taking off little slippers and socks and carefully covering Amy.

Cade's voice was a rough whisper. "Looks like they're done for the night."

Colleen bent down and kissed Amy's flushed cheek before she straightened and Cade quietly put up the side of the baby bed. They repeated the process with Beau in his room before they stepped out into the hall.

The big house was silent and empty. It was nearly ten o'clock. Esmerelda would be at home with her husband, but Colleen wondered about the nanny.

"Where's your nanny?"

"Fired."

Cade didn't remark on her surprise, but took her arm to start them through the house to the back patio. The night air was quite warm, but fresh. Despite the lights around the headquarters, the sky they could see from the open patio was thick with stars.

Cade spoke as they looked up at the sight. "If you agree to marry me, you can decide whether you want to hire a new nanny, or if you'd rather try out some of Esmerelda's teenage relatives to baby-sit or help

you with some of the kids' care. You know better
than anybody what you can handle and what you
can't.''

Colleen nodded because Cade glanced at her and
she knew he could see her in the dimness. His voice
went very quiet.

"I know I'm rushing you, Colleen, but once I
make up my mind, I rarely change it. I'm satisfied
we can have a respectable marriage that agrees with
both of us and gives the kids the stable family life
they need.''

Cade didn't wait for her answer. He turned to her
then and slid his arms around her to pull her snugly
against him.

And then he was kissing her. The warm night
wrapped around them and every breath she could get
was heavy with sensuality. Cade's kiss was so carnal
that she was helpless to keep from letting him control
her reaction. This time, she gave back, until Cade
finally broke off the kiss and they both stood shaking.

Her voice trembled but was audible. "I'll...marry
you."

The moment she said the words, her worries evaporated and a settled feeling smoothed away all but
the most faint ripples of doubt. That night, she slept
so deeply and so contentedly that she was certain
she'd finally found her place in the world.

Cade Chalmers was a human bulldozer, clearing a
path through a forest of obstacles and details. In four
short days, they'd got blood tests and a license, con-
sulted with her doctor and found a ring. Her personal
belongings and papers had been moved from her

apartment, and they'd signed the prenuptial agreement. Colleen had called a charity to donate her furniture, kitchenware and linens to, and they'd be picked up the next week.

She favored a very small, private wedding with the children in attendance, so Cade made it happen. Almost before she could register the passage of those few whirlwind days, she was standing with Beau and Amy at the foyer end of the aisle in the prayer chapel of a small country church.

She wore white linen slacks with a long jacket over a blue silk blouse that matched her eyes. Cade was impressive in his severe black suit. The stark white of his shirt set off his deeply tanned features, and his rugged looks were devastatingly handsome.

He'd bought her a beautiful bridal bouquet. It was a miracle of colors, from bright yellows to peach to pinks, a deep red, even a spot of purple and a very gorgeous and unusual blue.

Beau and Amy were adorable. Beau was dressed in a tiny suit that looked like a miniature of Cade's; Amy wore an impossibly frilly white dress, white tights, and white patent-leather shoes. She also had a tiny bouquet, almost exactly like the bridal bouquet, though Amy's flowers had been fastened to her chubby little wrist with a pale blue ribbon.

Colleen didn't know how Cade had found the time to shop for and select the children's new clothes, but he'd managed it somehow, along with everything else. Probably during one of her naps, when their mad rush had drained her and she'd simply been forced to rest.

The engagement ring he'd insisted she select was

the most beautiful she'd ever seen. The stunning white diamond was surrounded by a circle of smaller diamonds. It was like wearing a tiny galaxy on her hand. Colleen looked at it often, as much to assure herself that it was real as to see if she thought it was still as beautiful as the last time she'd looked at it. Which was usually only moments before!

If she'd lost her mind in the mad rush before the wedding, she hoped to never find it again. Happiness was not only within reach, it had engulfed her and her heart was both peaceful and turbulent with joy.

Now the organist began, and Beau and Amy escorted Colleen up the aisle to Cade. Beau held her free hand and his sister's, since Amy couldn't walk alone yet. Colleen's slow pace made it easy for little Amy to toddle along holding her brother's hand. Beau only lost his sister's hand twice, once coming up the aisle and once just before they reached Cade at the front.

Those times, Amy tumbled forward, catching herself on her hands before Beau grabbed her little waist and wrestled her upright to again start her in the right direction. It was hard to keep from giggling over Beau's cheerful and patient management of his wide-eyed baby sister.

When they'd reached Cade, Beau's spontaneous, "Here's our bride, Uncle Cade," made Cade chuckle softly as he took Colleen's hand. They both watched while Beau shepherded his sister to the front pew of the chapel.

Esmerelda and her husband Lorenzo seated Beau and Amy between them to witness the ceremony.

Together, Cade and Colleen turned toward the minister.

Cade held her cold hand warmly as the minister led them in the vows. Cade's "I do's" were gruff and grim; her own were soft, but clear.

Then Cade slid the wedding band on her finger and the sacredness of the moment descended. Her gaze lifted to meet the utterly somber darkness in Cade's as the minister pronounced them husband and wife. They'd completed one of the most serious acts of their lives. Colleen was deeply affected by it, and from the look on Cade's face, he was, too.

The words, "You may now kiss your bride, Mr. Chalmers," floated over them and Cade leaned down. His lips were cool and rigidly set. But the moment they touched hers, they relaxed and went warm.

It was over so quickly. A short ceremony with a few words, a pronouncement, a solemn kiss. And then they signed the certificate and collected their children as the photographer Cade had hired set up and organized them for several combinations of pictures.

The photographer was very professional and very efficient, managing the children's poses and theirs so quickly that neither Beau nor Amy became cranky or impatient.

By the time Cade settled them all, including Esmerelda and Lorenzo, in the Suburban, Colleen felt as if she'd just walked out of a beautiful dream. It had been such a small ceremony in such a small chapel, but each second of it was exquisite and precious to her.

Her prayer that her life with Cade and the children would be just as exquisite and precious for them as she hoped it would be for her, was a prayer she'd pray each day of her life from that moment on. Whatever Cade's objections to love, she was determined to see to it that he would never regret choosing her.

CHAPTER EIGHT

THERE was an uncommon amount of dust in the air as they turned onto the graveled ranch drive from the highway, as if several vehicles had recently driven over it. Esmerelda made a tsk-tsk sound from the back seat and Lorenzo murmured something quiet. Colleen couldn't help but notice that Cade's stern profile went a bit grim.

The moment they drove over the last rise of ranch road between the highway and the house, the reason for the excessive dust—and Cade's sudden grimness—was apparent.

Cars and pickups lined the drive near the house, which was virtually surrounded by more cars and pickups.

"What is this?" Lorenzo asked from the back seat.

Esmerelda supplied the answer for them all. "Someone has organized a welcome. Who has done this?"

Colleen glanced over her shoulder at Esmerelda's surprised face, then looked over at Cade. "A reception?"

Cade's terse, "Looks like," let her know that he'd had nothing to do with this. Colleen faced forward and watched as Cade pulled the Suburban to a stop at the end of the front walk. The spot had evidently been reserved for their vehicle.

Beau had unbuckled himself from his car seat and

now he leaned over the front seat between them, so excited his young face beamed with it. "We got a party!"

Cade turned his head and glanced at the boy's happy face. The disapproval Colleen had sensed in him suddenly slipped away, as if the boy's excitement had made him reconsider. He shifted his gaze to Colleen's. "Okay with you?"

Colleen gave him a wry smile. "I don't think we got a vote, but your friends must wish you well."

"They'll be your friends, too, Colleen. Might as well go in."

Whether Beau understood precisely what his uncle had said, he'd got the gist of it. So with an ear-splitting squeal of excitement, he drew back, scrambled over Lorenzo's legs and launched himself from the vehicle. Esmerelda took care of Amy.

Cade got out and came around to Colleen's side to open her door and help her to the ground. He placed her hand in the crook of his arm and they walked to the door. By that time, Beau had already been in the house, but now he came running back out.

Several of the guests filed out behind him and the front veranda was suddenly crowded. Just as Colleen and Cade stepped into the shade, a chorus of congratulations went up. Cade stopped, then passed Colleen's cane to Beau before he swept her up in his arms. He carried her over the threshold to applause, but continued to the living room where two chairs had been set at one side of the room for the bride and groom.

Beau trotted along after them and handed Colleen her cane once she and Cade were seated together.

Esmerelda carried Amy and handed her to Cade before she rushed away to see who had invaded her kitchen.

The tall, elegant blonde Colleen had seen the first day she'd come to the ranch, stepped out of the crowd and came toward them. The room went quieter, which got Colleen's attention.

The blonde was so beautiful that the sight of her was breathtaking. She had the self-assurance of a model and the carriage of a queen. Her honey-gold skin was flawless, and her tousled hair was thick and rich with gleaming waves.

The white sundress she wore was tight and provocative enough to make her look bosomy, and her long, tanned legs were as showy as the rest of her. She was as perfect as a Miss America, and Colleen doubted that anyone in the room would disagree.

The contrast between the blonde's sultry perfection and her own plain looks and too slim boyish body made them complete visual opposites. Colleen felt slightly dizzy at the thought that everyone around them would be making the same mental comparison.

The blonde had eyes only for Cade, and as she stopped in front of him, Colleen was near enough to be engulfed in the same musky cloud of fragrance as he was when the blonde ignored her and little Amy to lean down to him and plant a swift kiss on the hard line of his mouth.

The only emotion Colleen was capable of suddenly was sharp jealousy. The feeling shot roof-high when the woman straightened, then reached down to Cade's mouth to whisk a smudge of bright lipstick off his lower lip with her thumb.

The easy familiarity of the gesture jolted Colleen. Her gaze went instantly to Cade's, but his dark eyes were fixed on the blonde.

Was that anger?

Colleen couldn't mistake the ominous glitter in his eyes and she felt profound relief. Cade was angry about that kiss. *Very* angry. Colleen chided herself for her swift jealousy. Cade had no doubt had several women in his life. This one was apparently among that number.

When the blonde suddenly turned to look at Colleen and briskly introduced herself as Angela Danner, Colleen could tell the woman heartily resented her. Those jewel-blue eyes made a slow sweep of her face, then slid lower, the faint curl at one corner of her lush mouth telegraphing her scorn.

She didn't give Colleen enough time to finish a polite response to her self-introduction before she turned dismissively and strolled away like a woman confident that the faint sway of her shapely backside was a magnet for male eyes.

It gave Colleen fierce satisfaction to see that Cade had stood up to shift Amy to his other arm and offer a handshake to the elderly gentleman who'd been waiting for an opportunity to greet him. Cade hadn't spared a second's glance at Angela Danner's retreat, though the elderly man hesitated a few moments to do just that.

All was well. Then the guests moved forward in small clusters to meet her and she forgot about Angela Danner.

*   *   *

Cade had many friends, neighbors and business associates who held him in enough esteem to accept a last-minute invitation to an impromptu reception for him and his bride. Colleen was touched by that and very proud to be married to a man who was so well thought of.

No one claimed responsibility for organizing the reception—complete with a four-tier wedding cake and refreshments that not only included food but also champagne. The only dark note that afternoon was that Angela Danner's behavior later on became something less than mannerly, when she drank to excess and her father, a white-haired oil man who'd barely spoken a word to Cade or Colleen, quietly took her home.

It seemed to Colleen that everyone seemed more comfortable after that, particularly Cade. Her instant acceptance among the guests was very moving for Colleen. Over the course of the afternoon, she learned that Cade had been the target of romantic speculation for years and that he'd been the cause of more than one fit of palpitations.

He'd become reclusive after his brother's death this past month, and people who knew him well had become concerned. When some of the talk in quieter corners of the house descended to gossip, Colleen overheard bits and pieces about Cade's mother, whom it was said had wronged his father and been neglectful of her sons.

Cade had mentioned the woman his father had married, but Colleen had assumed he'd been talking about a second wife. There had been no second wife. The woman whom Cade declared had not been worth a minute of his father's time, had been his own mother! Coupled with his knowledge of Craig and Sharon's troubled marriage, it was no wonder that he was so resistant to the notion of love.

Several of the guests expressed their delight to her that Cade had found a wife to make him happy after Craig's tragic death. And though they'd understood the private wedding, it was taken as a sign that Cade was ready to resume a social life, hence the surprise reception from people who wished him well.

As Colleen made the rounds, many expressed belated condolences to her about Sharon, as well as their best wishes for Colleen's happiness with Cade and the children.

To her relief, no one made a reference to Sharon beyond the fact that her death had been a tragedy that Craig had never got over. And no one made the comparisons between her and Sharon that she'd grown up with, not even the less obvious ones of "Sharon's so beautiful, you don't look related."

Colleen had made so many new friends that the thrill of it helped her defeat the weariness of the long afternoon.

Cade had been managing the children while she was distracted meeting the guests. Later, she found out that Beau and Amy hadn't been able to settle down enough to take naps. Once the children had grown so tired, Cade had handled them with his usual gruff affection, tolerating the fact that they'd both wanted him to hold them on his lap and carry them wherever he went.

He'd been the soul of patience and still was. Amy now rested her head on his wide shoulder with her fingers in her mouth; Beau either sat beside Cade with his small arm linked with Cade's, or got grumpy and insisted on being carried when Cade went off to socialize in another part of the big house.

By the time Colleen stood on the front veranda and tossed the bridal bouquet, both children were so whiny and out of sorts that she felt guilty for not taking them for their naps herself.

Just as the last of the guests bid them goodbye and best wishes, Amy fell asleep on Cade's shoulder and Beau was barely able to keep his eyes open. Both children had eaten their way through a hefty share of the reception food, so they needed naps worse than they needed an early supper.

Together, she and Cade took the children to their rooms. Cade went with Beau and Colleen managed the sleeping Amy after he'd laid her gently in her bed. Colleen had taken off Amy's sweet little dress and was carefully washing the sticky remains of cake and punch off her face and tiny hands when Cade came in.

He gripped her shoulder gently. His whispered, "You're tired, baby. Let me finish up," made her heart fill with sweetness.

There was little more to do than spread a light blanket over the little girl before Cade put the side of the bed up. Then he turned to her and slid his big hands around her waist.

"One more to put to bed," he said, his mouth angled into a smile. "Today wasn't what I'd planned, but was it all right with you?"

Colleen's heartfelt, "It was perfect," deepened his smile and he leaned down to sweep her into his arms.

She managed to keep her cane and hold on as he strode quietly from the room. He carried her briskly down the hall to the very end, then through the door to his room.

To her complete surprise, Cade joined her for her nap. She'd felt only a few moments of intense self-consciousness, but it vanished the moment he gave her a simple, gentle kiss. There was no passion in it, but she sensed that was deliberate because she was so tired. She turned slightly away to lie on her side and Cade settled snugly behind her.

It felt so heavenly to lie with her head pillowed on Cade's upper arm and her back pressed against him, that she couldn't fall asleep immediately.

Cade rubbed his big, hard-palmed hand on her hip in lazy, soothing circles. His breath gusted over her ear and cheek. All he'd had to do was touch her and her body responded, relaxing, then going slack with the pleasure of contact. Emotion welled up and her eyes went damp. She'd never be alone again.

The fresh realization of that couldn't have impacted more deeply than if she was realizing it for the first time. She hesitantly touched Cade's arm and stroked his forearm with restrained affection. Her voice was a choked whisper.

"Thank you for today."

Cade heard the emotional undercurrent in her soft voice. He reckoned that was the mark of a woman who'd had so few good things in her life that she treasured whatever good came her way. The thought caused a peculiar turbulence in his chest.

He recalled the scene she'd described with her father and his girlfriend, how she'd told him the story in a small, quiet voice, almost as if she was still that child who'd been forced to sit at the table and not speak.

Then she'd humbled him by softly declaring that Beau and Amy would grow up thinking he'd hung the moon. That told him better than if she'd said straight-out that she'd been badly disillusioned. Cruelly, in his judgment.

Now he understood why Sharon had been so manipulative with Craig, so determined to have everything she could get, so incapable of thinking about anyone but herself. Why she'd almost seemed to delight in working Craig into a lather of anger and frustration.

Colleen was Sharon's complete opposite. She should have been a bitter, grasping little bitch, out to make the world pay for her pain. But she was soft-hearted and kind. And sweet. So sweet.

It dawned on him then that he might be on the verge of slipping past "like" into emotions he'd vowed to refuse. In seven short days, Colleen James—Colleen Chalmers now—had dragged him shockingly close to the precipice.

How had she got him so far? Maybe the more honest question was, why had he allowed it?

Even he heard the warm affection in his rough, "Get some sleep now." At least he'd kept from adding *baby* at the end of it this time.

But it felt so unnatural not to use the endearment that he pulled her even tighter against himself in silent apology. His body tingled and went hot, but he told himself that the heavy pulse of his blood was merely lust. That if he hadn't felt Colleen's small body slowly relax into exhausted slumber, he might have been able to distract himself from weightier thoughts by initiating her into carnal pleasures that didn't require anything stronger than sexual attraction and opportunity.

The peculiar turbulence in his chest—and the lust he felt—was frustratingly slow to subside.

Neither of the kids slept very long. They'd gotten too tired before their naps, so they were restless. And so cranky when they got up to have supper that neither child was happy about the food Esmerelda had prepared.

After supper, Colleen and Cade took them for a walk, hoping the fresh evening air would put them back in better humor. Beau wanted to throw rocks, so they walked up the driveway and let him do it. Amy rode quietly in her stroller, mollified at last.

The day after she'd agreed to marry him, Cade had asked her if she'd like to have a honeymoon. He'd offered several choices, but Colleen had asked to delay it. Since they'd married for the sake of the children, it seemed to her the best thing would be to give them time to adjust to the sudden change in their lives.

They all needed a chance to develop a regular routine. In the last few days, they'd been so consumed with her move from San Antonio and organizing the wedding, that everything had been disrupted.

Colleen was particularly grateful now that Cade had agreed to her request. These past days had been wearing and she was still a little in shock. Seven days ago, she'd endured the traumatic drive to the ranch to speak to Cade and ask to be part of the children's lives.

Now she was married to him and starting a new life that was so radically different from anything she'd ever imagined for herself that she wouldn't have been too surprised if someone pinched her and told her to wake up.

The magnitude of what they'd done rose in her soul and roared over her. A terrible feeling of panic chased close behind, and she suddenly felt afraid.

"Colleen?"

As if Cade was so sensitive to her that he'd sensed her terror, he caught her arm and brought her to a halt.

"Something wrong?"

Colleen glanced anxiously at his rugged face, then away. She had to give him some answer, because he was obviously concerned. She made herself smile, but the effort felt unnatural.

"T-the first car I ever bought was just a cheap thing, not very fancy. Just three thousand dollars. I didn't have much money left over after I paid for rent and the basics, but I was sure I could afford the payment because I'd got the car loan for as long as they'd allowed. Lots of interest, but really low payments each month."

Now she glanced nervously at him and suddenly felt a little sick that she'd started to tell him this. Cade Chalmers had a luxury car, an SUV, and a multitude of ranch vehicles. All bought new. Once they were worn out or he tired of them, he probably traded them off or sold them. And any one of those vehicles would easily get him far more than a measly three thousand dollars in either trade-in or sale. She felt her face go hot.

"And?"

Cade was taking the story seriously. He was almost grave about it, and that made her squirm inwardly. No doubt she sounded very naive and inexperienced. And poor. Desperately poor. She'd done far better for herself financially after that first car purchase, but compared to Cade's wealth...

The sick feeling was overpowering, but he was waiting for her to finish, so she had no choice but to go on.

"The m-minute I got in and started it up, I was suddenly...scared to death. I was terrified I'd miscalculated. That when I got home and added everything up, I'd realize I wouldn't be able to afford the payments. But I'd signed a paper promising to pay every month until the loan was done. And what if it broke down and cost too much to fix? W-what if..."

Cade was watching her, she could feel the pressure of his gaze. When she finally had the courage to look at him to see his reaction, she almost couldn't keep her eyes on his face long enough to see what it was until he spoke.

"Buyer's remorse." Now his solemn expression eased, and a smile stretched over his mouth. His gaze was sparkling with kind humor. "Or in this case, marital remorse."

Colleen's breath gusted out on a fresh wave of nerves. "This is worse."

Now he chuckled softly. Beau came skipping back to them from the small distance he'd got when the two of them had stopped for the story.

"What's funny, Uncle Cade?"

Beau was in far better humor and he was smiling now, too.

"Grown-up stuff, squirt. You keepin' those rocks out of the grass?"

Beau gave a nod. "Yup. Only on the road like you said."

"Good boy. Why don't you push your sister's buggy back to the house?"

Beau made a face. "Ah, now?"

"Dark's coming on," Cade said firmly. "You and your sister need a bath." He reached out to gently ruffle the boy's hair when he made another face about the bath.

Beau obediently took hold of the stroller and awkwardly turned the small vehicle toward the house. They followed the children and Cade's arm came around her to keep her against his side. His voice was low in the warm twilight.

"Don't worry about the payments on this marriage, Colleen. And if some of this is wedding night jitters, I think I can fix those, too."

Colleen glanced quickly at his face and saw the lazy promise in his dark gaze. Her skin prickled with heat and anticipation. For all Cade's sensual tutorials these past days when they'd had a few moments of complete privacy, intimacy was still a mystery. She knew the clinical aspects of sex, but having never experienced it herself, she was nervous and more than a little worried about it.

Flustered, she looked away. Cade's arm tightened around her.

"We've only been around each other a week,

baby. I mean to seduce you, but I don't have a deadline.''

The gruff promise managed to both ease her tension and send the anxious feeling of heat and anticipation soaring.

Far sooner than Colleen expected, they finished with the children's baths and dressed them for bed. Because Beau and Amy were still tired from the long day, both went quickly to sleep.

Colleen was somehow energized by the nervousness she felt. Cade had gone to his office in the other wing of the house, and she'd loitered in the living room, pretending interest in a news program before she'd given up and gone off to Cade's bedroom.

Their bedroom now. Just that morning, Esmerelda had helped her move her things from the guest room she'd been using. Her modest collection of clothes now hung in the huge walk-in closet on a rod opposite the one that held Cade's clothing. Her plain lingerie was folded away into one of the four empty drawers reserved for her on one side of Cade's wide dresser, and her toiletries took up an empty drawer and a tiny corner of a shelf in the huge master bath. Her small collection of jewelry sat in a small, velvet-lined box on the big dresser.

Her belongings seemed few and were virtually nondescript among Cade's. Thin shadows that barely left a mark on the masculine possessions that dominated Cade's private rooms. Colleen felt just as small and nondescript, and it was suddenly terrifying to realize that she might never be more than a thin shadow in his dynamic life.

And yet she was married to him, waiting for him in his huge, handsomely appointed rooms, expecting him to walk in very soon and join her. And they'd share his big bed.

Too restless to wait placidly, she collected her nightclothes and fled to the bathroom for her shower. The hot water soothed some of her tension and she reminded herself at least a dozen times that Cade had told her he'd set no deadline.

We've only been around each other a week, baby.

Baby. He'd been gentle with her so far, so very considerate. And whenever he called her baby, she felt so protected, so...cared for. He understood that she was sexually inexperienced and very nervous about it. Surely she could trust that he didn't expect a true wedding night right away. He'd as much as said so, hadn't he?

We've only been around each other a week, and *I don't have a deadline.* Not precise statements, but certainly clear enough that she could take comfort from them, couldn't she? She had when he'd said them, so why couldn't she now?

Probably because she knew in her heart that no matter how much better she came to know Cade, she would be just as nervous her first time, whenever it might be.

Later, she stood in front of the wide mirror over the counter in the master bath, freshly showered and dressed in the floor-length white cotton nightgown and robe she'd bought that week. Her eyes looked as big as dinner plates, and her still-damp hair was softly tousled then lightly spritzed with something to make it behave, yet kept it soft to the touch.

She looked impossibly virginal and vulnerable.

I mean to seduce you...

The rough-voiced words still made her tremble. The physical contrast between Cade's blatant masculinity and her own fragility was enough to weaken her with a peculiar dread that was half fear, half thrill. And then the insecurity she'd suffered her whole life sent the peculiar dread straight into dry-mouthed terror.

She was so much less than a man like Cade should have had to settle for. He was a man who'd planned to never marry, but he'd changed his mind because the children needed the normalcy of two parents in a stable home. He was sacrificing so much for them and getting precious little in return.

Marrying Cade was no sacrifice for her because he was giving her the universe. He was getting a plain wife, a co-parent for the children, but a co-parent who still needed almost as much care as they did. A wife who'd need to have help—probably often his—with the daily care of Beau and Amy, a wife who couldn't yet be a full companion in his active live, a wife without the stamina to do much caring for a husband.

And a wife he might soon see as a burden because she had physical limits that might interfere with his workday. He'd been so solicitous of her, so accommodating. But her father'd had no patience with his wife's illness and had quickly divorced and abandoned her.

Cade was not like her father in any way, but how patient would he be if she couldn't take full care of the children very soon? He'd told her she could hire another nanny or Esmerelda's nieces, but how soon would it be that he'd expect her to be able to handle Beau and Amy with no outside help?

Cade's long delay coming to bed and her deepening weariness multiplied her worries about the future.

What if Cade became impatient with her early bedtimes and her naps? She was often restless at night and every single morning she woke up to muscle spasms that were sometimes painful enough to bring tears.

She'd shunned muscle relaxers because she was terrified of the addiction her mother had suffered with painkillers, and she hated that the pills practically knocked her out. But would she have to reconsider because Cade's sleep might be disturbed or cut short?

Her brain was whirling with it all. She'd asked herself these questions before, but now that they'd gone through with the wedding, somehow each one had become earth-shatteringly important, their answers less certain and more potentially disastrous.

Just then, she heard Cade come into the bedroom. A handful of heartbeats later, the sound of keys and change hitting the heavy crystal dresser tray as he emptied his pockets made her reach shakily for her cane. He'd want a shower, so she shouldn't make him wait.

Colleen took a deep breath to steady herself and opened the door. She tried to blank the worry from her face and prayed for success before she stepped through the doorway onto the plush carpet of the big bedroom.

CHAPTER NINE

THE moment Cade saw his new wife, his good intentions evaporated in a blazing flash fire of lust. Colleen's face was flushed from her shower, but shyness sent her soft color soaring. She wore a white floor-length cotton robe over a white nightgown that was probably just as modest and concealing.

She looked so fragile and feminine, and so completely untouched and virginal that something harsh and fierce and primitive in him was compelled to claim her. To claim her and mark her and hoard her to himself. *Tonight.*

This minute.

He saw the panic that streaked through her pretty eyes and felt instant remorse. He didn't understand the power of his feelings, so he was damned sure she wouldn't. They must have shown on his face however, and going by her flash of panic, they must have looked just as fierce as they'd felt.

Cade made himself smile gently and was rewarded when he saw her panic ease. The answering tremble of her soft mouth wasn't much of a smile, but the effort touched him.

He'd never slept with a virgin, but suddenly he was aware that he was the only man Colleen would ever have. If she stayed with him. In the future, every attitude Colleen would have toward sex would be set by their first time.

And Colleen was his wife. He'd stood in a chapel that day and taken vows with her. It struck him now that sex would never be the same for him. There was a new dimension to it suddenly, something more profound. His brain shied from the word "sacred" and picked out "special."

Sex with Colleen would not be just a joining of male and female, but of husband and wife. And not for only a time or two, but from this night on, time after time, year after year, with one woman. This woman.

This shy, gentle, fragile, very vulnerable woman. Colleen was an innocent. It was up to him to give her something in return that was worthy of that innocence, worthy of her.

The responsibility was staggering suddenly, but not staggering enough to make him back down. His blood was already thick with desire. His body was heavy with it, both heavy and restless. He knew he'd given her the impression that intimacy could be postponed, that he'd not set a deadline. He'd said words to that effect, but perhaps it was just as well that the sweet sight of her had changed his mind.

If he was careful, if he was tender, she'd never regret this and neither would he. His decision made, he held out his hand and let her see a glimpse of what he felt in a soft smile.

"Come here, Colleen."

She hesitated a moment, then moved forward. She was trembling, but when she was close enough, she reached for his hand and let his fingers close warmly around hers. He caught a hint of determination in her blue eyes and realized that this was hard for her.

Like a stroke of bright lightning he realized she was struggling to trust him, to comply with his wishes even if she was afraid of what they might be. He pulled her gently that last step to him, slipped her cane from her fingers and set it on the dresser before he pulled her close.

Cade's hands settled on her waist and Colleen felt an earthquake of feeling go through her. He leaned down slowly, but instead of kissing her, he nuzzled the side of her neck. His lips were warm and unhurried, almost lazy. Colleen couldn't help that her tension began to melt.

His voice was a low rasp. "Trust me, baby."

He continued to explore her flushed skin with his lips, her neck, her ear, her jaw. Everything in her clamored for his lips to move to hers, but instead they skated away, back to the tender flesh below her ear before he nudged aside the shoulder of her robe and nibbled gently.

She felt the light weight of the robe slide to her elbows and realized dimly that Cade was removing it. She could barely stand without the cane. Once the robe dropped to the carpet, her hands came up shakily but no longer had the strength to grip his wide shoulders. Cade stepped backward and she fairly floated along with him as his strong hands guided and supported her.

The room shifted and whirled as his lips moved onto hers, and she found herself beneath him on the bed. His mouth slid off hers to sear her flushed skin as he hovered closely over her; his lips brushed everywhere, lingering, roaming and making her tremble with sensation. Her breath went shallow and her blood moved heavy and hot.

She was insensible after that, so overwhelmed and drugged with the pleasures Cade lavished on her that later she barely felt the sting of pain. It was a small pain, instantly forgotten, blotted out by each incredible moment of pleasure that followed. Until the breathless intensity of it all carried her so high that her body was somehow luminous with sensual splendor before it burst into shards of white light and rained back to earth in a sparkling shower of joy.

Colleen got carefully out of bed that next morning, quietly moving around the room to gather her clothes and a few toiletries before she escaped to the bathroom in the guest bedroom to shower and dress for the day.

It was so early that the sky was only beginning to lighten, but the muscle spasms that began her mornings had started and she'd wanted to walk them off, then shower and dress without disturbing Cade's sleep.

It had been painful to make herself slip out of his arms, to force herself away from the pleasure and security of his big body. Before that, she'd had only a few seconds to savor the feeling before discomfort compelled her to leave.

Once she'd walked off just enough of the spasms and the stiffness, she quickly shed her robe and stepped into the shower in the guest bath. She directed the hot water to her legs, hoping the heat would soothe the sharp ache.

She wasn't ready to face Cade yet. A lifetime of

shyness and modesty had been breached. Cade knew things about her body that she hadn't, and he'd used that knowledge to incite her response. A response that in the dim light of early day seemed far too wild and abandoned to have been hers. What had he thought? Would she see disappointment in him today? Disapproval?

Though she hadn't considered herself totally naive, it amazed her now that she'd never imagined sex could be quite like...that. Had she really been so ignorant? Cade's very skillful initiation had not only enlightened her, but he'd created in her a hunger for more that made her feel even more vulnerable to him.

The word "sex" seemed so stark and impersonal. Last night had been neither of those; there'd been only tenderness and consideration. And pleasure. Heart-stopping and intense, with an obvious affection that, in retrospect, seemed almost...worshipful. Could she have been mistaken?

If Cade hadn't made love to her last night, if it had only been sex, then she wasn't certain she would ever understand the difference.

Colleen finished with her shower, applied a few cosmetics, then combed and lightly spritzed her hair with a holding mist to set the soft, so-short style before she dressed in the gray cotton blouse and jeans she'd brought in with her. A soft rap of knuckles on the closed door startled her and she stepped over quickly to open it.

Cade stood just outside, dressed for the day in a blue-and-white striped shirt and once-dark jeans worn soft by hard use. His dark hair was still damp from his shower, he was clean-shaven, and his rugged face was sternly set. His gaze however, was gentle.

The power of his masculinity—and what she knew about it now —sent a longing through her that took her aback. She couldn't keep her wide gaze from taking him in, couldn't keep it from moving over him from head to boot before she finally caught herself and managed to look at his face.

Heat climbed high in her cheeks and she glanced away, suddenly so self-conscious about last night that it was almost painful.

"We've got a shower in our room. Why use this one?"

She heard the faint disapproval quite clearly. "I didn't want to wake you."

"We'll be waking each other for years to come, Colleen. I'll adjust."

Her gaze skipped back to make contact with his and he added, "You'll adjust to me."

Now she saw the heat in his dark eyes and a tremor of weakness went through her. He lifted a hand to her face and touched her cheek with the calloused pad of a finger. The avalanche of pleasure nearly made her knees buckle.

She stepped forward to the welcome in his arms and his lips were on hers. She was nearly incoherent by the time his mouth eased away. She opened dazed eyes to see the soft fire in his.

"Never know when we might like to start our days the way we'll be ending them."

The remark was a firm promise and Colleen's worries about what Cade thought of her after last night vanished. She had no sense that she'd disappointed him in any way beyond the fact that she'd not used the shower in their bathroom. *Their* bathroom, *their* room. He'd made himself very clear and it was exactly the low-key reassurance she'd needed after last night.

We'll be waking each other for years to come, Colleen, was a promise of security. Colleen felt the first strong stir of true confidence.

Cade eased back a step and took her hand. "Let's get some breakfast before the kids wake up."

Colleen stepped into the bedroom and they walked together to the kitchen.

To her surprise, Esmerelda's three nieces arrived before they finished eating. Cade introduced Carmen, Rosalie and Angelina, then informed Colleen that they'd be taking care of the kids that morning.

He also told her that there was no need for them to wait at the house for Beau and Amy to wake. The riding lesson Cade had delayed until after the wedding would happen that morning while it was still early and reasonably cool.

Colleen was nervous, but didn't protest. The gelding he'd mentioned was not the horse he ended up having her ride that morning. Instead he saddled a showy little pinto mare with brown markings over her snowy-white coat. The mare was very gentle and sweet-tempered, inquisitively nuzzling Colleen's hand and inspecting her cane.

"Changed my mind about the gelding," he told her. "The mare's smaller and smoother gaited."

Cade demonstrated how to saddle the mare, explaining the reason for each step until he finished and let down the stirrup. When the moment of truth came, Cade confiscated her cane and lifted her to the saddle. He handed her the mare's reins, but kept a cautious hand on a leather lead he'd snapped on the mare's bit.

He patiently adjusted the stirrups then coached her on proper body posture and how to hold the reins. Too soon he walked the mare out into the early sunlight, keeping track of Colleen and giving an occasional instruction or comment. After she seemed more comfortable, he let out the lead so Colleen was more directly in control.

She rode the pretty mare—Chica—little more than twenty minutes, but when they arrived back at the stable for Colleen to dismount, she literally couldn't manage it. Once Cade lifted her down, her legs refused to support her at all, so she sat on a hay bale while he unsaddled the mare.

Instead of putting Chica back in her stall, he led the mare outside and turned her into one of the shaded corrals. By that time, Colleen had regained her feet and walked out to join him before he could come back for her.

"Still shaky?" he asked as she reached him.

"Not bad," she said then smiled. The ride had stretched and used muscles she wasn't accustomed to working, but she felt good about the ride. Chica was a sweetheart and she was surprised to realize she was looking forward to the next ride.

Cade returned her smile. "First time's hard on the legs for most folks, Colleen. But they'll get stronger. Probably faster than your regular therapy. I've got a good liniment, so speak up if you could use some."

"I'm fine right now."

"Good. I'd like to drive you around some of the place. We'll see if the kids are up, let them know we haven't run away from home, then we'll take my truck." He smiled again. "We'd better scare up some sunblock and find you a hat."

They walked back to the house then and Colleen was amazed to realize she felt energized. Later, nothing spectacular or particularly novel happened that morning as Cade drove her around the ranch, but Colleen began to feel the beginning of a deep closeness between them.

Though she needed a nap as badly as Beau and Amy after lunch, the rest of the day was just as peaceful and satisfying as that morning. By supper, Colleen had sent Esmerelda's nieces home, and she and Cade spent a quiet evening with the children before they gave them their baths and put them to bed.

When they were alone again in their room, Cade barely closed the door before he reached for her. The tender passion she'd craved all day seemed even more deep and meaningful then than it had the night before.

She lay in his arms later on, overwhelmed. But for all Cade's tenderness and passion, there'd been no love words.

And though she knew Cade didn't mean to love her, she wondered how long she could keep silent about her feelings for him. It didn't seem possible that she could have fallen in love with him so quickly, but she had and what she felt for him was deepening by the moment. How would he take it if she told him she loved him?

The inevitable fears and insecurities rose up, and she wasn't certain she'd ever be brave enough to take that risk.

Those next days and weeks were the most idyllic of her life. She was with Cade and the children every day, and every moment she spent alone with her husband was exciting and wonderful. The nights she spent in his arms were particularly sweet, and whether he loved her or not, his lovemaking made her feel loved. Cherished.

Her heart opened so fully to him that she was amazed she was able to keep silent, but she was worried that a clear confession of love from her might spoil it all.

Instead, in those next days and weeks while Cade returned to daily work on the ranch, she focused on relentlessly pushing herself, providing the majority of the care for Beau and Amy. She was determined to do as much as possible for them herself, but she couldn't lift or carry Amy, so getting her into or out of bed was a challenge.

Diaper changes were even bigger challenges, since lifting Amy to her bed or a changing table was unsafe. Kneeling on the floor to do it was too hard on Colleen's knees, so she taught Amy to accommodate her by climbing onto one of the sofas.

Colleen's praise when Amy lay quietly or her sometime use of an interesting toy to occupy the child, seemed to solve the problem. Besides which, Colleen learned to change diapers in record time so

Amy's patience with the process usually lasted long enough.

And though Amy was often content to play quietly in the house, Beau was a bundle of energy. He couldn't spend all of his time indoors, so Colleen spent hours at a time outside so both children could benefit from outdoor play in the fresh air. The heat was exhausting until she began to adjust.

Amy learned to walk quickly after that, and she toddled along under her own power. The three of them went with Cade often to watch the work on the ranch or to look over the stock.

Afternoon naps were taken on the floor with the children, using cushions she and Beau pulled off the furniture in the playroom. Colleen kept the playroom door closed during the naps, afraid that one or both children would awaken before she did and wander off.

Cade usually came in just before supper. Bath time at night was a joint project with both children in the same bathtub. Cade bathed Beau and Colleen managed Amy. Rocky the dinosaur and a vast assortment of other tub toys made the time fun and messy, but it wouldn't be long before the joint baths would have to cease.

After the children were dried and dressed in their sleepers, it became a regular ritual for the four of them to sit together on the living room sofa for bedtime stories. Cade corralled both children on his lap and Colleen sat leaning against his side to read aloud. She rarely read a book through to the end a second time before both children were asleep and she and Cade put them to bed.

Colleen got to know more of Cade's friends and neighbors at Amy's first birthday party. And they went to court to officially adopt Beau and Amy, which prompted another celebration. Colleen decided to accept the trucking company's settlement offer, which took care of her lost wages and medical care, as well as a substantial amount besides. Cade's financial advisor helped her decide how the large sum would be handled.

In fewer weeks than she'd have believed possible, the early rides she and Chica went on with Cade had indeed strengthened her. She walked now without her cane, and though she couldn't skip rope or run marathons, she was so much stronger that she'd recovered an ease of movement that approached what she'd had before the wreck.

Her stamina after those first exhausting weeks, when she'd pushed herself so hard, began to increase until naps became a sometime event. In those next months, she gained weight and her hair got longer. Her skin carried the same healthy glow that seemed to illuminate her soul, and she realized she was almost pretty now. Cade Chalmers' effect on her life had been sweeping and profound.

It became harder than ever to keep back the words she most wanted to say to him: *I love you.* Simple words, heartfelt ones, but words that might spoil everything if he didn't want to hear them from her. And yet they burst up in her heart so frequently now that they were often the next words on her tongue. Several times, she'd come within a syllable of speaking them but something always held her back.

What if she was worried for nothing? Cade was

perceptive enough to have long ago guessed what she
felt for him. He'd not done a single thing to discourage her displays of caring and affection toward
him, and he'd held nothing back from her.

Nothing but the words.

In the end, she became convinced that she couldn't
keep worrying about it. Surely he wouldn't be surprised when she told him she loved him, not when
he'd done everything possible to ensure it.

It was during one of their early rides together that
she brought it up. She'd made arrangements for
Esmerelda's nieces to be at the house all morning,
so there was no pressing need for her to get back for
the children.

She'd ridden out with Cade to a spot within two
miles of where he planned to work that morning with
his men. He'd meant for them to ride directly to the
meeting point, but she'd asked him to detour to one
of the creeks that cut through the ranch.

It was one of her favorite places, though only a
trickle of water moved through the sandy creek bed.
They surprised three deer, who scampered off and
disappeared into the early dimness, probably in
search of a cool resting place to shelter them from
the heat of the late summer day.

The eastern sky had just bloomed into a gorgeous
sunrise of vivid pinks, subtle oranges and gold, so
Colleen pulled Chica to a halt on the creek bank to
enjoy it. Cade rode up beside her and his big bay
sidestepped to brush Cade's leg against hers.

She glanced over at him, saw the curiosity in his
dark eyes and felt her courage waver. She was so
completely in love with him that just a glimpse of

him was precious to her. She loved the low, gruff sound of his voice and lived for even a simple touch from him.

Had he really drawn a line with her that he'd never cross? And was his line, his boundary, meant to keep her from crossing over to him? In the end, whatever his objection to falling in love, he was a good man and an honorable one. He was careful of the children's feelings and he'd been careful of hers. Surely that wouldn't change.

She tried a small smile and the curiosity in his eyes deepened.

"That's an 'up-to-something' smile," he said sternly, but the sternness on his face and in his voice was canceled out by the sparkle of humor in his gaze.

Colleen put out a hand and Cade took it. His fingers closed warmly on hers. She took a shaky breath and made a cautious start. "You've given me so much."

Sudden emotion silenced her and she fought to keep her stinging eyes dry. Cade's expression went grim and the sparkle of humor ebbed slowly to solemnity, as if he sensed what was coming.

She felt an odd strangling sensation. "I don't know where I'd be if you hadn't invited me into your life, if you hadn't been willing to share Beau and Amy." She hesitated again when his solemn gaze wavered from hers. "I know what you told me about the red hearts and flowers kind of love, that you won't ever feel that way, but I—"

Cade glanced away from her then and she cut herself off. She watched as his profile went stiff. She felt it when he closed himself to her, and she was stricken with hurt. And though she was terrified now, she didn't stop.

Maybe she could make him understand why she had to tell him this. Maybe she could coax him out of his terrible grimness. Maybe...

"After everything you've done, all the sweet, caring things, I'd have to be made of rock if I didn't love you. In fact," she said, her voice going shaky from the pressure of emotion, "I don't think it's possible for another woman anywhere to love a man more than I love you."

Her soft voice trailed away in the early morning air. The utter stillness in Cade was truly ominous now. His dark gaze was fixed on the bright horizon as if he'd been deaf to every word she'd said. His fingers were suddenly cold and she felt the pain to her soul when his grip went slack and he released her hand.

His voice was low and gruff. "I'll be out till about noon, then I've got business in Austin. No tellin' if it'll be a day or the rest of the week."

A wave of dizzy shock rolled over her and she could barely breathe. "Please, Cade, don't do this."

He seemed oblivious to her soft plea, but the way his thumb fidgeted with the reins was the only outward clue that he was deeply upset. He went on quietly as if she hadn't said a word.

"You probably need to get back for the kids."

Colleen stared as Cade simply turned the bay and rode off. He didn't look back as his big horse moved into a gliding trot, then into a gallop. Her heart was beating so erratically in her chest that she felt dizzy and sick. The sensations were so strong that she clung to the saddlehorn, not certain she could stay upright. Her shocked brain refused to focus on anything but a panicked review of every terrible moment, every terrible word.

Somehow, Chica got her back to the stable. Esmerelda's nieces agreed to stay the rest of the day, so Colleen spent a few minutes with the children before she retreated to the master suite to wait out the dizzy sickness that had escalated and now included a sharp headache. She was too shocked and ill to cry, but she craved the refuge of sleep.

A few aspirin and a nap took care of the worst of her headache. The dizziness had abated by the end of the nap, too, but she recognized the heavy sickness as grief. Feeling too fragile to wait around and face Cade this soon, she spent a few minutes playing with Beau and Amy, hugged them long enough that they squirmed with impatience, then told Esmerelda she'd be spending the rest of the day shopping.

The long ride to San Antonio was remarkable because she felt nothing more than a whisper of unease when she met a semi. She had no idea what to shop for when she got to a mall, but her main task for the day was to get used to the idea that her life had changed again, and this time, not for the better.

CHAPTER TEN

CADE knew he'd overreacted. Colleen had caught him by surprise, though he shouldn't have been surprised. A woman didn't look at a man the way Colleen looked at him—she couldn't respond to his touch like Colleen responded to his—unless she was in love.

Her actual words had surprised him anyway. He'd not wanted to hear her say "I love you" because it was too risky to say it back to her. The guilt of staying silent had blindsided him, tying his gut into knots and yanking hard. Riding away from her had done nothing to ease it, and his conscience had pounded him mercilessly every minute since.

Cussedness made him work that morning, but no matter how hard the work, no matter how many bitter scenes from his father's life and his brother's marriage that he'd made himself replay in his head, it hadn't been enough to smother the knowledge that he'd wronged Colleen. He'd resisted her words and then hurt her by coldly riding away, as if he'd so totally rejected what she'd said that he'd rejected her.

If he'd been thinking more clearly, he'd have grabbed her off her saddle, kissed her senseless, then carried her off someplace private. Hell, he could have had her right there on the creek bank. She wouldn't have noticed until later that he'd never said the words. And when she remembered, she'd accept that

166

he would never say them. She wouldn't have been traumatized, she wouldn't have been hurt.

His conscience pummeled him with fresh vengeance for that lie. Colleen would have been hurt by his silence anyway, no matter how differently he'd handled things that morning.

By noon, sharp anxiety drove him back to the house. Why had he held out so long, why hadn't he gone after Colleen hours ago? Hell, why had he ever left her there on the creek bank in the first place? The picture of her shattered expression and stricken eyes made him feel sick.

The moment he hit the door, Esmerelda was speaking to him in rapid-fire Spanish and it took him a moment to mentally make the switch to follow her. When he did, the sweat that sheened his face and dampened his armpits had nothing to do with hard work or the heat.

Colleen had spent the morning in bed, then gone shopping for the day in San Antonio. Esmerelda hadn't understood that she'd meant to leave immediately—or without Cade—until a few minutes ago when she'd realized that Colleen had already left the house.

It had been months since Colleen had been behind the wheel of a car, so it was odd for her to drive so far alone. Or to make the sudden decision, particularly when Esmerelda reported that she'd looked shaky and pale, even after a morning in bed.

Esmerelda had been trying to contact him on his cell phone, which he'd inadvertently left in the den that morning. She'd given up and had been dialing his foreman when he'd walked in.

Cade dashed to his office for his cell phone, grabbed the keys to the Suburban, then rushed out of the house. Colleen was forty-five minutes ahead of him, but she'd probably drive well below the speed limit, since she was still leery of having a wreck. If she wasn't feeling well, her terror of driving might cause her to pull off someplace, so he'd keep a sharp watch. With any luck, he'd either find her within the first handful of miles, or he could outdrive her and catch up.

Colleen found herself parking on the street in front of her mother's old house in a rundown neighborhood in San Antonio. The paint was just as faded and peeled as it had been when they'd lived there, though Colleen knew it had been painted in the more than six years since she and Sharon had moved away. The front porch was crooked, the lower panel on the storm door had been kicked in, and a crack in one of the front windows had been patched with duct tape.

But the shabby little house was still standing, was still habitable enough to provide shelter for people too poor to take proper care of it.

Some of the bleakest times in her life had been spent in that house. Her mother's first bout with serious illness had happened there when Colleen was ten years old and Sharon was eight. Their father had divorced their mother and abandoned them by the time Colleen was twelve. Their mother had been awarded the house in the divorce, but the payments had been difficult to meet because their father had sent child support only frequently enough to keep his wages from being garnished.

Her mother's inability to keep jobs long-term had been due to her illness and the long series of treatments she'd gone through each time there was a recurrence. Colleen had virtually raised Sharon, so it had been Colleen, not their sick mother, whom Sharon had rebelled against as a teenager.

To Sharon, who'd been desperate to be popular and "cool" in middle school and high school, Colleen had been the dowdy, repressive big sister who'd nagged her to do her chores and discouraged her from hanging out with boys.

That mother-daughter sort of conflict had carried over into adulthood. Sharon had died still immature enough to feel as embarrassed by her lackluster older sister as teenagers often were by their uncool parents, which was why Sharon had so seldom invited Colleen to the ranch. And, she'd surmised, Sharon was wary of her disapproval, so the less Colleen really knew about her life with Craig, the more comfortable Sharon was.

Sharon's quick marriage to Craig Chalmers at eighteen had been her attempt to escape the poverty and pain of their upbringing. Sharon had escaped the poverty, but she'd never escaped the pain.

As Colleen stared blearily at the old house, other bad memories came back. One of the most difficult times had been when she was sixteen. She'd handled the finances for her ailing mother for years by then, and the bank was threatening to foreclose on the mortgage.

Her mother had been fighting another battle for her

life and Colleen was desperate to keep her from giving up. She'd been terrified of what it would do to her mother to lose her house. In the end, Colleen had sacrificed her one true success—as an honor student—to drop out of school and go to work full-time.

For the next year and a half, her mother believed she was going to school every day, and Colleen had gone to great pains to let her go on thinking that, until the day came when their mother became too ill to be aware of anything. It was almost the only time Sharon had cooperated with her back then, and that one bit of cooperation had lasted until their mother passed away the month before Colleen turned eighteen.

Within six months, Colleen had sold the house, and she and Sharon had moved to an apartment in a better neighborhood so Sharon could finish school. After Sharon married Craig, Colleen had gotten her G.E.D., then taken accounting classes at night to find a better job.

Coming here today had been a necessity. The hell she'd lived then had seemed interminable at the time, a horror without end, where "normal" and "stable" couldn't get a toehold and her life had been ruled by crisis after crisis. And she'd been so young to have gone through all that, so young to have found that kind of courage.

Other than Sharon's death and the aftermath of the wreck, nothing else had ever seemed nearly as bad or bleak or hopeless as the years they'd lived here.

The fresh reminder eased the shock and agony of those terrible moments with Cade today. She'd survived her years in this house, so she could survive whatever was ahead with Cade. However intimidating he could be, nothing he was capable of would be so much as a smudge mark on a corner of what she'd lived back then.

The fact that she'd sought out such an extreme example to put her troubles with Cade into perspective suddenly seemed silly to her, though it had been effective. Cade Chalmers was no monster. His reaction today had a logical explanation, whether he'd ever confide it to her or not. Surely there was some way to fix things or to at least reach some sort of compromise.

Cade was rigidly determined to give the children a stable, loving home with two parents. And since nothing short of death would devastate Beau and Amy more than divorce, she was safe from the idea that Cade would easily banish her from his life.

That at least gave her a chance. In fact, she had a fairer chance with Cade and better odds for success than she'd had any of those other hard times.

Peace eased through her then and she felt the hurt of that day lose its power. She dried her eyes and reached to buckle her seatbelt. She put the idling car into gear and checked the street before she pulled away from the curb and started back to Chalmers Ranch.

Both children came running into the entry hall when Colleen walked in. She crouched down for hugs and smiled at Carmen and Angelina who'd followed. Rosalie, they reported, had gone home earlier because a boy she had a crush on was coming to their house to return a borrowed tool to their father. The girls had giggled over that and the happy sound lifted her heart.

Before Colleen could respond, Esmerelda came bustling in, a look of concern on her face.

"Señor Cade has been searching everywhere for you," she said urgently.

Colleen released the children and straightened. "Does he have his cell phone?"

"*Sí.* I called him when you drove in. He is very upset."

Colleen's gaze veered guiltily from Esmerelda's. "I'm sorry. I didn't mean to cause upset. Have the children had their supper?"

"*Sí.* I fed them early, as Señor Cade said."

Colleen didn't remark on that, though she was surprised. She and Cade always ate supper with the children. She glanced at the girls. "Thanks for keeping them today."

Esmerelda spoke before the girls could answer.

"Señor Cade asked them to take the children for the night to their house. My sister is pleased to have them stay, so there are no worries." Esmerelda smiled at Beau who had grown excited at the reminder of the overnight visit. "They will have a good time with the other children."

Colleen was shocked by that news, but the girls didn't notice, chattering about the things they'd packed so Colleen would know they'd be taking plenty of bottles and diapers for Amy and enough clothes for both children. She gave a distracted nod. The girls had always taken care of the children in this house because Cade didn't approve of the kids going anywhere without her or him.

For Cade to suddenly allow it now—for him to arrange it without consulting her—increased her unease. Once Esmerelda went home for the night and the girls took Beau and Amy with them, she and Cade would be alone. But alone for what? After what had happened that morning, it would be foolish for her to assume this was some sort of romantic plan.

The courage she thought she'd found—the wild hope—drained away so swiftly it was as if she'd imagined it. Feeling a little queasy, she looked over at Esmerelda. "I'm sure they'll have a good time, but do you know why he's doing this?"

Normally Colleen would never think to ask Esmerelda such a question, since it might put the housekeeper in a position that could strain her loyalty to Cade. It wasn't fair to do that, and she regretted it immediately.

"You don't need to answer that, Esmerelda. I shouldn't have asked."

The gently sympathetic look the housekeeper gave her made her glance away, suddenly anxious. She'd immediately noted the fact that Esmerelda didn't rush in with words to the effect of, "Don't worry, the boss is not angry with you." In fact, it seemed that Esmerelda was very eager to whisk the children out the front door to her car while the girls rushed to get the bags they'd packed.

Esmerelda was apparently leaving for the day then, too, she realized, probably so she could drive the children to her sister's house. But something about Esmerelda's haste and the girls' rush, gave the children's night away from home an odd significance that deepened her anxiety. And they hadn't spent a night away from her the whole time she'd been married to Cade, which made it worse.

Colleen stood at the open door, seeing the children get into Esmerelda's car with Carmen and Angelina. Her children were being swept away. *Quickly* swept away. Already she ached to hug them again, but Esmerelda had started the car. Her impulse was to run after them and bring them back, but she was leery of vetoing Cade's orders.

In the end, it was the surprising pain of seeing Esmerelda's car drive away that made her decide. She had to get her kids. She'd just turned to get the keys she'd tossed to the entry table when she heard the staccato sound of the Suburban's horn, and glanced back to look out the open door.

The big black vehicle had just crested the last rise to the main house. Cade had apparently sounded the horn several times in rapid succession as a greeting to Esmerelda and the children. But Colleen wasn't certain how he'd had time to see Esmerelda's car on this side of the rise and honk like that, because the Suburban was rocketing up the ranch road to the house so fast she was surprised it wasn't airborne.

Panic made her back away from the door. She was suddenly shaking. Cade was driving like a maniac, and she'd never once seen even an inkling of that before. He was always so calm and controlled behind the wheel. It had to mean he was furious.

But why would he be furious? Surely not because of what she'd said to him that morning. And he'd encouraged her to take the car and go shopping several times in an effort to get her to drive again. She'd done that today. Though the reason she'd finally done it had nothing to do with driving or shopping, he'd repeatedly coaxed her to do it.

And, she'd left the children in good care with a promise to Esmerelda about when to expect her back, which she'd met. Cade had told her he was going to Austin, so he shouldn't even be at the ranch.

The illogic of it all made things so much worse, and she realized she was letting herself get too upset, too frightened. Her knees were so spongy now she could hardly walk. But walk she did, to the living room and the kitchen then through the sliders to the paved stones of the patio.

She stopped there and paced, willing herself to quit shaking, mentally scolding herself for being so unreasonably terrified. Cade had never so much as raised his voice to her, but then, she'd never seen him truly angry. She'd long ago stopped being intimidated by his gruffness because he'd never used it to even faintly threaten her.

But then she remembered his harsh expression that morning and the way he'd looked away from her, suddenly deaf to her words. He'd closed her out so completely that the memory still shocked her.

She jumped when she heard the roar of his voice as he entered the front door. The sliders were closed and the house was large. To hear her name so loudly from out here on the patio rattled her even more.

"Colleen!"

She heard the heavy thud of his boot heels as he stalked out of the living room into the kitchen then across the tiled floor to the sliders. She turned shakily to face the doors, her heart beating wildly. He loomed on the other side of the glass like a surly giant, coming to a rigid halt the moment he saw her standing outside.

Oh, God, he was so angry-looking, so big, so hard-edged and powerful. His big hand swiped the sliding glass aside, the movement so effortless for him that the heavy door might have weighed little more than a fly.

His face was like weathered rock, but she caught the faint surprise that quickly registered on it. She all but flinched when his turbulent gaze sharpened on her face, then sliced over her trembling body before it returned to meet hers.

The furious rigidity in his big body seemed to slacken fractionally and she felt herself able to take a breath. Now he stepped through the open door but stopped the moment she swayed slightly.

"Colleen?" His big voice was suddenly low and gravelly, as if she was a colt that could be easily spooked. His sharp look gentled. "You worried me half to death, baby."

Baby. The name she loved, the name he only spoke with affection. It was the signal that she truly had let herself get too upset, that she'd terrorized herself. Her eyes stung with relief.

Suddenly ashamed that she'd thought the worst, she jerked her hands up to press her fingertips against her cheekbones and the sides of her nose, so close to tears that only the pressure of her fingers could help hold them back. She made herself smile in a desperate effort to enforce her determination to not break down.

"You're so...angry," she got out. "I don't understand why."

Cade's stern expression abruptly went soft and she saw the pain that shot through his gaze and caused his dark brows to angle into somber whorls. His voice was a quiet rasp. "I was worried to death about you. Esmerelda said you were in bed all morning, then you suddenly left the house to drive to San Antonio."

Colleen drew in a careful breath, as much to help her control the sting of tears as to breathe. She couldn't lower her hands yet and Cade's gaze seemed to take somber note of that.

"I was just…upset. I h-had to ..think. Never meant to cause worry Thought I had the ki-ids taken care of. Didn't think you'd mind. S-sorry."

She stopped, mortified that the effort not to cry had made mincemeat of her explanation.

"I didn't mean to scare you, baby."

God, she loved the low, rough timbre of his voice, loved the way it stroked her insides and made her feel warm and adored. The tears pressed harder, so she did, too. "I'm glad." A tear popped over her lash and shot onto her trembling fingers.

Cade walked toward her then, and the man who might truly be able to snap his fingers and make the planets realign held his big work-hardened hands out to her.

Colleen moved forward suddenly, as if his body was a magnet. She all but flew into his arms and cried out with helpless relief when they closed fiercely around her and he lifted her against him. She hugged him just as fiercely, soaking the shoulder of his shirt with a deluge of tears, relieved beyond words that it had been this simple.

When she could catch her breath and find her voice, it was a raw whisper. "I was terrified I'd spoiled it all."

Cade's arms tightened and he burrowed his lips against her shoulder. "You didn't spoil a damned thing, baby, not a damned thing. I promise."

The emotion in his voice sent a poignant ache through her and she squeezed her eyes more tightly shut in an agony of helpless love. She held on as she felt Cade reach down to lift her thighs so her legs were wrapped around his hips. His arms came back around her and she felt him walk across the patio to their room. The whisper of cool air registered as he carried her past the door, but the heat of their bodies pressed so tightly together kept her from feeling the chill.

He was kissing her before he could kick the door closed behind him. Colleen held his head between her hands, kissing him wildly, grateful beyond words that the crisis had passed. She would live with this resolution. She would be happy with it because she couldn't bear the alternative. Their estrangement that day had proved it to her.

Cade was the one who pulled back and she was painfully sensitive to any hint of withdrawal. She opened wet-lashed eyes to see his face. Cade's hand came up to her cheek.

"We've got to settle some things, Colleen."

The solemn words caused a quiver of dread, but then he gave her a faint smile that seemed sad to her. She saw the weary pain in his dark eyes and felt a strong pang of sympathy.

Cade walked to the armchairs grouped near the

French doors. When he loosened his arms, she slid down the front of him to her feet. She took a step back, but he caught her hand to keep her close. She looked up at him, saw his stony expression and the bleakness in his eyes. He started with his usual bluntness.

"My daddy was crazy in love with my mother," he said roughly, and she heard clearly the bitter way he'd said *my mother*. "She mighta loved him once, but it burned out quick. The harder he worked to make her stay, the crazier he got. He used everything to keep her with him, but she played him for more. Damned near bankrupted the ranch to satisfy her, but when the cash ran out, so did she."

More than the words, the harsh anger and stark pain on Cade's somber face shook her. His gaze wavered from hers, then dropped. As if he realized they were still standing, he eased Colleen back a step to one of the armchairs.

She sat and he crouched down in front of her. He stared a moment at her feet, then reached for her ankle. It was as if he couldn't look at her, but needed some small ritual to help him contain his emotions. He gently lifted her foot and methodically stripped open the Velcro tabs on her shoes. She felt the faint tremor in his hands.

"Broke his health trying to build the ranch back up," he went on.

The story was obviously hard to tell. Cade's father had actually sold off chunks of the ranch that had been in his family for generations. It couldn't have been easy to get those back and it had taken years. Cade's mother and father had been divorced long before then. Rebuilding the ranch had been complicated by his mother's returns. She'd call or come by, hinting at reconciliation, and his father had been so eager for that and so grateful to hear from her, that he'd let her leech a little more from him each time.

Because she'd never stayed, his father would go on days-long drunks, deeply depressed and threatening to shoot himself. Cade and Craig had hidden every gun on the ranch to prevent that, and when one of them couldn't watch over their father, the foreman had the task.

Cade finally pulled off her shoe and set it aside to reach for her other foot. But he didn't open the Velcro tabs, he simply held her foot and stared at her shoe. Colleen kept completely still, compelled to watch every nuance of feeling on his face. But it was as hard-set as rock, though she could see the deadness in his downcast gaze. His quiet voice sounded almost robotic then, as if he was lost in the bitter memories.

"Wouldn't listen to good sense. His next biggest regret besides the fact he couldn't get my mother to stay, was that he died when he didn't mean to. Cold sober of a heart attack the first morning of spring roundup. His last words were about her, begging me to go find her so he could see her one last time."

He managed to start on the tabs, and Colleen saw his struggle to come out of the memory. That was when she realized his startling bluntness now was a cover for deep pain. As if he had to tell the story as harshly as he did to somehow keep his pain at a distance.

"Wasn't worth a dollar he gave her or a minute of his life. Craig was the same kind of crazy, followed our daddy's path right into the bottle. Rode out to the highway one night, drunk. Ended up five miles away, he and his horse drowned in one of the neighbor's creeks. He knew better than to pull a stunt like that, so it maybe wasn't a true…accident."

Colleen sat, a little in shock at Cade's grim conclusion. He finished with her shoe and pulled it off to set it aside. Long moments went by as his thumb brushed absently over the top of the foot that rested on his wide palm. When he looked up, her heart ached at the haunted darkness in his eyes.

"Other than the normal fears for the kids' safety and health and upbringing, I didn't think I was afraid of anything anymore. Found out today I've been a coward all along. A coward too set in his mind to see he's unreasonable."

Colleen searched his dark eyes, trying to understand this because Cade Chalmers was no coward. But what he'd told her about his family explained so much. His insistence on the prenuptial agreement and his scorn for what he called the red hearts and flowers kind of love, made complete sense to her now.

"I wanted a common sense marriage," he went on, a little more recovered from the melancholy of seconds ago. He set her foot down and braced his fist on the arm of her chair. "I made a good choice in a wife and I was satisfied. More than satisfied."

The way his voice had dropped to a whisper at the end gave his words an added tenderness that made her ache with love for him. Her heart began to lift then and she felt the first radiant glimmers of hope.

"But a common sense marriage makes no sense when you find out you love your wife, but you're afraid to face it. When she tells you she loves you, all you can think about is that if you say the words back to her, you'll give her the power to cut your heart out piece by piece until there's nothing left."

Colleen could barely breathe. Cade reached for her hand and gripped it. "But this woman isn't like those others and you realize you've believed the wrong things about love all your life. And you've been so damned self-righteous about it that you've taken out your fear and bitterness on her."

Cade's grip tightened. "She's such a sweet wife, gentle and loving. She's made your life full and rich. She smiles and you feel peace. If there's any woman in this world who's worth being crazy in love with, it's her."

The huge lump that was choking her made her eyes fill. She spontaneously reached to touch his hard jaw. He caught her wrist and turned his head to press a kiss in her palm. His eyes squeezed closed, as if he felt desperate gratitude. His voice was a warm growl against her skin.

"I'm sorry, baby, so sorry."

Now he opened his eyes and looked at her, still pressing her palm to his face, rubbing it against his skin as if he savored the feel of her touch.

Colleen managed to speak. "I understand now." Her words were barely audible. "Thank you."

"I love you, Colleen." He'd said that in a hushed voice, as if those words were sacred. "I probably fell in love with you when you first came to the ranch. The day I realized we had to marry, I told myself it was for the kids. But the truth is, I had to marry you quick so I wouldn't have time to think."

Colleen lifted her other hand to tenderly cradle his rugged face between her palms. Cade reached for her and as he straightened, he pulled her to her feet with him and kissed her.

The incredible tenderness of his hard lips made her achy and breathless. The careful, seeking pressure was magic, and her heart clamored with feeling. She drew back only enough to look up at him.

"I love you so much, Cade. You'll never be sorry, I promise."

Cade kissed her lightly and she felt his words against her lips. "I promise, too, baby. You'll never be sorry, I *swear* it." His gruff, "I love you, Colleen," made her joy bubble out in a delighted laugh.

Cade drew back a little, his answering smile handsome and relaxed. He lifted her, his arms tight around her waist, to turn them around and around until they ended up on the bed, laughing, touching each other, gently teasing, then pulling at clothes as desire rose as high as their dizzying joy. They lost track of everything then but each other.

When at last they lay together, warmly entwined in the dim, quiet room, it wasn't long until they loved again. After that, they drifted peacefully to sleep.

And sometime in their dreams, each glimpsed the

sweet faces of the little ones whose lives would join theirs in the years ahead. Little ones who, along with Amy and Beau, would happily expand the Chalmers family, until the west wing of the big ranch house was fully occupied, and the Chalmers' legacy became one of love and joy.

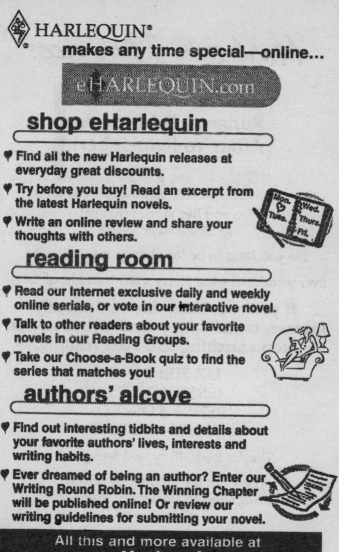

Harlequin Romance ®

EXTRA!!! The Times EXTRA!!!

Runaway Bride Seeks Affair To Remember!

Do you like stories that get
up close and personal?

Do you long to be loved *truly, madly, deeply*?

Ever wondered what Harry *really* thought of Sally?

**If you're looking for emotionally
intense, tantalizingly tender love stories,
stop searching and start reading:**

LIZ FIELDING
JESSICA HART
RENEE ROSZEL
SOPHIE WESTON

They're fresh, flirty and feel-good.

Look out for their latest novels,
coming soon to Harlequin Romance®.

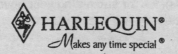

HARLEQUIN®
Makes any time special ®

Visit us at www.eHarlequin.com   HRRS

A brand-new story of
emotional soul-searching and family turmoil
by *New York Times* bestselling author

Penny Jordan

Featuring her famous
Crighton family!

STARTING OVER

Focusing on the elusive Nick Crighton and his
unexpected exploration of love, this richly woven story
revisits Penny Jordan's most mesmerizing family ever!

"Women everywhere will find pieces
of themselves in Jordan's characters."
—*Publishers Weekly*

Coming to stores in October 2001.

HARLEQUIN®
Makes any time special ®

In October 2001
Look for this
New York Times bestselling author

BARBARA DELINSKY

in

Bronze Mystique

The only men in Sasha's life lived between the covers of her bestselling romances. She wrote about passionate, loving heroes, but no such man existed...til Doug Donohue rescued Sasha the night her motorcycle crashed.

AND award-winning Harlequin Intrigue author

GAYLE WILSON

in

Secrets in Silence

This fantastic 2-in-1 collection will be on sale October 2001.

What happens when you suddenly
discover your happy twosome is about
to be turned into a...*family*?
Do you laugh?
Do you cry?
Or...do you get married?

The answer is all of the above—and plenty more!

Share the laughter and the tears with
Harlequin Romance® as these
unsuspecting couples have to be

When parenthood takes you by surprise!

THE BACHELOR'S BABY
Liz Fielding (August, #3666)

CLAIMING HIS BABY
Rebecca Winters (October, #3673)

HER HIRED HUSBAND
Renee Roszel (December, #3681)

Available wherever Harlequin books are sold.